PISTOLS AND PETTICOATS

BOOK 2 -
MISADVENTURES OF THE
CHOLUA BROTHERS

MAGGIE MAGOFFIN

Author Credits: Reliving the Past Old Time Studio
Logo Artist—Nan Wright

ISBN: 978-0-9909-4253-5 (sc)
ISBN: 978-0-9909-4254-2 (e)

Because of the dynamic nature of the Internet, any web addresses or links contained in this book may have changed since publication and may no longer be valid. The views expressed in this work are solely those of the author and do not necessarily reflect the views of the publisher, and the publisher hereby disclaims any responsibility for them.

Maggie M. Publications

Nan Wright

Rev. date: 08/05/2015

Now all glory to God, who is able, through his mighty power at work within us to accomplish infinitely more than we might ask or think.-Ephesians 3:20 NLT

Tailing Tales of Colorado

The golden yellow piles of debris referred to as *tailings* seen along the mountainsides of Colorado are much more than mere piles of waste rock and dirt. Many hold potential treasure yet undiscovered.

Just as those *tailings* hold such treasures, I hope my stories bring to you a treasure-trove of never before told tales and historical facts you find informative and entertaining.

Maggie M

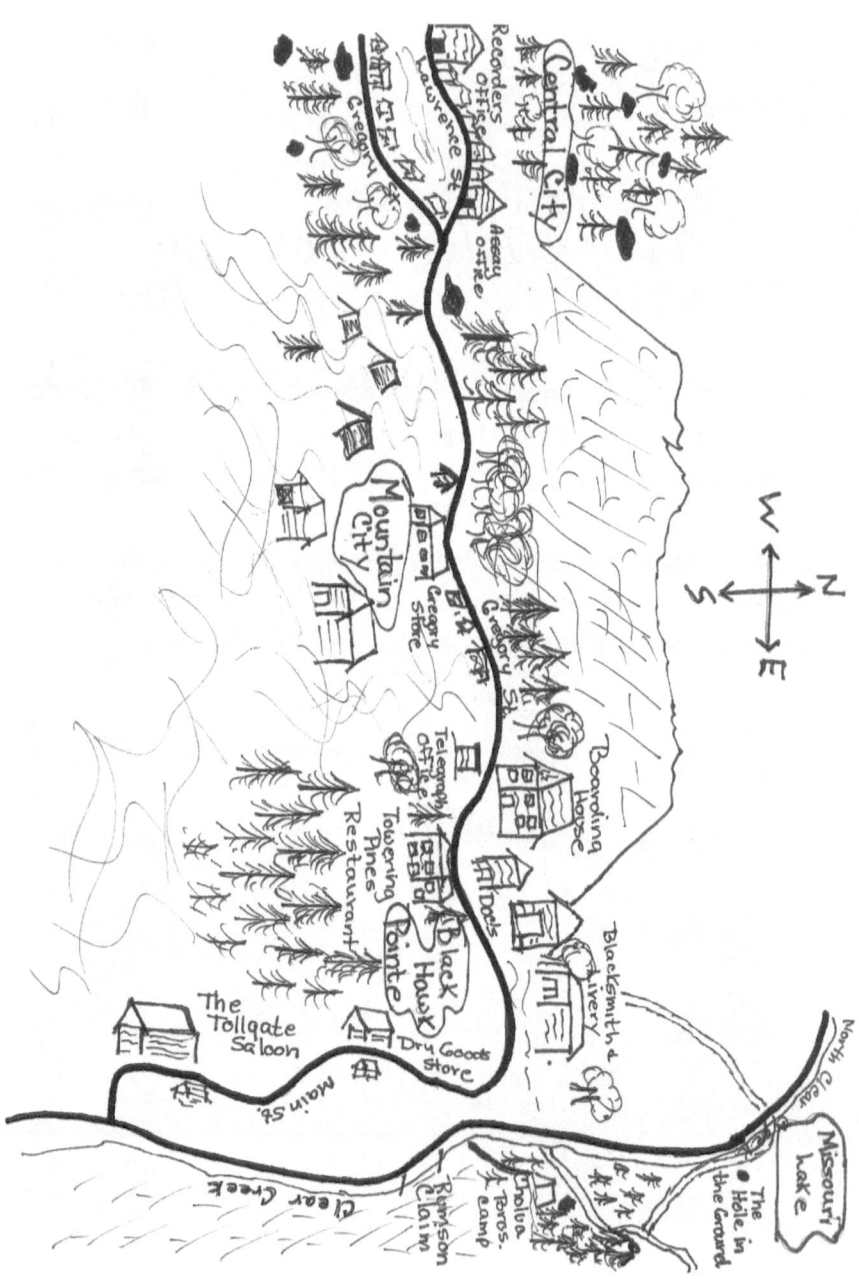

CHAPTER

Black Hawk Pointe, Colorado
September 1860

The store clerk lowered his eyes and shook his head. "Ma'am, it just ain't somethin' you need to know. I found his body lyin' in the creek up yonder. Why you wanna go askin' me to tell you more?"

Victoria Cashman laid her hand on his. "I need to know how he died."

"Did you know Mr. Rumson?"

"Yes, I knew him quite well, and it is essential I know the details of his death." She swallowed past the lump in her throat. "He and I were . . . we were quite close."

The clerk turned his back to her and arranged cans on the shelf. "I'm sorry, ma'am. I understand you needin' answers. The plain fact is, I can't see how knowin' the gory details of the man's death is goin' to help you." He turned around and braced his hands on the counter. "Just leave it be! He's dead and that's that."

"Can you tell me who buried him?"

He exhaled. "I took him to the undertaker up in Central City. Might be you could talk to him."

Victoria bid the merchant a cursory thank you and then hurried from the dry goods store to the blacksmith shop. She peered inside the open doorway. The forge stood cold in the dark, empty room. She pulled her wrap tightly around her shoulders and shivered as she passed through to the livery. Uncertain if the chill came from the damp cold or apprehension. She shouted, "Anyone here?"

A boy with freckles and disheveled blonde hair stepped from the shadows. "Yes ma'am. Can I help you?"

Victoria inhaled a quick breath. "I need directions to the undertaker in Central City—and I need a horse and buggy."

The boy rested his weight on the handle of a pitchfork, a somber frown crossing his face. "Somebody die?"

"Yes."

"Recent?"

"No. Several weeks ago."

The young man shrugged. "So why you need an undertaker now?"

"I was told he could tell me what I need to know."

"Who was it died?"

His sweet charm and sincere curiosity reached a place in Victoria's heart. She softened her approach. "You ask an awful lot of questions."

"Yes ma'am. Mr. John—He be the blacksmith—well, he told me, 'Timmy. If you wanna learn anythin' in this life, you gotta ask questions.'"

She laid her hand on his small shoulder. "Did Mr. John also tell you it is not polite to be nosey?"

He hung his head and muttered, "Sorry. Didn't mean to be nosey. The last feller I know died 'round here was that Rumson feller, and it seemed nobody cared that he died."

The news that no one cared that Ben had died pained her but did not surprise her. He had a way of irritating people. "Did you know Mr. Rumson?"

Timmy straightened. "Yep, sure 'nough did."

"And you know the details of his death?"

He shrugged. "Ain't no secret. Everybody was talkin' 'bout it."

Yes, everyone had been talking about the murder of Ben Rumson. However, who knew the truth? Rumors and gossip were getting her nowhere. "Can you tell me what you heard, Timmy, and who told you?"

His eyes grew wide and he gave a toothy grin. "Oh, yes ma'am! Mr. John, he done seen the body and I heard him and Mr. Dane talkin' 'bout it. They said somebody done shot him plumb through the back of the head, and when that bullet come out of his face it done tore his nose right off."

Victoria's stomach lurched at the thought. Nevertheless, Timmy's account of the horrid incident made more sense than any other story she had heard. He continued with animated gestures, occasionally raising the pitch in his voice. His chatter was only an echo in her consciousness. The young man's hand gripping her arm brought her out of her musing.

"You okay, ma'am?"

She stuttered, "Yes—I'm—sorry."

"You plumb went pale on me." He motioned toward a rough-hewn wooden stool. "Maybe you ought to sit a spell."

She patted his small, dirty hand, still gripping her arm. "No. I'm fine. Thank you." She forced a smile. "Do you know when Mr. Rumson was killed?"

Timmy scrunched his lips as though deep in thought. "I'm thinkin' they said somethin' 'bout Sam—He be the bartender at the Tollgate—Mr. Dane said somethin' 'bout Sam seein' Mr. Rumson the night before. So I'm guessin' he couldn't a been lyin' in the creek more than a day when they found him." He shrugged. "Just sayin' that's what I figure."

In spite of his tattered clothing and filthy condition, Timmy radiated a youthful, joyous glow. Yet, his eyes held a maturity and sadness Victoria was unable to ignore. She looked around the livery and then back at Timmy. "Do you live here?"

"No ma'am. I live with my ma."

It was a relief to know the boy was not an orphan. "And your pa?"

He shook his head. "Pa was killed in a minin' accident last year. It's just me and Ma."

Victoria brought her gloved hand to her chest. "Oh, Timmy, I'm so sorry. It must be painful for you to talk about."

Timmy shrugged. "Oh, it's okay."

"Where do you live?"

Timmy pointed up the hill. "We got us a tent up near Mountain City."

Her sister, Ruby, and she had taken a room at Miss Maggie's boarding house until the renovations on the building Victoria purchased were completed. She could not imagine living in a tent in this mountain climate, especially during the winter months. Moreover, there was little honest work for women in a mining camp. "What does your mother do while you're here at the livery?"

Timmy chuckled. "You ask an awful lot of questions."

She laughed. "I am sorry. I'm really not being nosey. It's just that you're such a sweet, well-mannered young man that I'm curious to know more about you."

"Naw, it's okay. I was just joshin' with you. Ma does laundry, and cookin', and whatever else folks will pay her to do. We get by."

Cooking? Victoria had been searching for a cook and had nearly given up hope. There were few women in the area. None of the men, even if they could cook, was likely to be willing to work for a woman. She pressed her hands together and smiled. "Oh, Timmy, that's wonderful. I'm opening my restaurant in a few weeks and I really need a cook. Could you please ask your mother to stop by Miss Maggie's and see me?"

Timmy nodded in a rapid motion. "Oh, yes ma'am. I'm sure she'd like that, and she's a real good cook."

Victoria turned to leave. "Wonderful! I look forward to talking to her." She stopped and turned toward Timmy. "By the way, what is your mother's name?"

"Angela. Most folks just call her Angie."

"Well, I hope to speak with her soon."

Timmy cleared his throat. "Ma'am, can I ask one more question?"

"What is it?"

He scuffed his worn boot in the dirt, his eyes downcast. "What's your name?"

She laughed a loud guffaw, and she brought her hands to her lips. "Oh my, Timmy, I am so sorry. How rude of me. My name is Victoria Cashman." She laid her hands on his shoulders. "You may call me Miss Vicki."

Timmy grinned. "Okay, Miss Vicki. You want me to get that buggy ready for you?"

She shook her head and sighed. "No. Thank you, Timmy."

CHAPTER

2

Two Weeks Later
The Towering Pines Restaurant
Black Hawk Pointe, Colorado

Victoria wiped a streak from a pane of glass in her newly installed window, grimacing at the sight of the ominous gray clouds and snowflakes falling softly onto the muddy street. One week after opening, her restaurant had become quite popular with locals and travelers passing through. The onset of an early winter storm would keep people from traveling and reduce her profits greatly.

Two well-dressed men entered through the front door. Victoria tucked her cleaning rag in the pocket of her apron and hung the garment on a hook in the back hall. Checking her hair in a large oval mirror, she went to greet her customers. "Gentlemen, welcome to The Towering Pines." She pasted on a sweet smile that grew wider with recognition of the handsome man standing in front of her.

She laid her hand on the man's arm. "It can't be. Is it really the Cholua brothers come to grace my fine establishment?"

Dane Cholua tipped his brown felt hat, revealing thick black locks. His blue eyes sparkled, and he quirked his lips in a smile. "I believe you promised us a meal."

"I hardly recognized you. Quite a change from the last time I saw you."

A younger and lighter-haired version of Dane faced her. Sweat dribbled down this man's temple as he pulled at the collar of his shirt and removed his black felt hat. "Is Ruby here?" he said in almost a whisper.

Dane glared at his younger brother. "Please forgive my manners, Miss Cashman, this is my brother, Jake. I don't think you two have met. But, it seems he's takin' a likin' to your sister."

Victoria grinned. "It's nice to me meet you, Jake. Ruby mentioned meeting you at The Tollgate, and I'm sure she'll be glad to see you again. She's upstairs. I will let her know you are in the restaurant. I am certain she will want to stop by and say 'Hello.'" She directed her attention to Dane. "Would you like a seat by the window?"

He tugged on the lapel of his jacket. "That'll be fine."

After seating the brothers and taking their order, Victoria hurried into the kitchen and ladled up two bowls of cream of potato soup. She returned to the dining room, and set the china bowls in front of the men, along with silver spoons and linen napkins. "Angie makes amazing soups. I hope you'll enjoy it while she prepares the rest of your dinner."

The brothers each picked up a spoon and, with their faces nearly buried in their bowls, they began slurping. Dane stopped eating and raised his eyes to Victoria. "Sorry. It's been a while since we ate with ladies around. You must think we're a couple of heathens." Sitting upright, he laid his napkin on his lap, dipped his spoon into the soup and then brought the spoon to his lips. "It is mighty good soup."

"I'm glad you like it." She looked at Jake, who continued slurping with his face to his bowl. "It appears your brother likes it as well." She giggled. "I do like a man with a healthy appetite."

Jake raised his eyes toward Dane and then faced Victoria. Soup dripped down his chin. "Yes ma'am, mighty good soup."

Victoria returned to the kitchen, occasionally peeking around the corner of the open doorway to watch Dane Cholua. She eavesdropped on their conversation.

The younger brother continued tugging at his stiff, white collar. "Don't know why we had to spend all that money and get all duded up just to come to dinner."

Dane shushed his brother. "It ain't killin' you to dress up once in awhile. Ma would have a fit if she knew how we been livin' and dressin' these past months."

In the kitchen, Victoria set a serving tray with plates and silver while Angie prepared the main course. Timmy's mother had been a true godsend. Blonde, and petite, quiet and unassuming, the woman went about her duties with no complaints. She cooked the men's steaks to a medium rare and added fresh peas and carrots on the side. Victoria arranged the food-laden dinnerware, and two crystal glasses of water on the tray, and carried the meal out to her customers.

Jake's jaw dropped as Victoria placed their meal before them. She stepped back from the table and her heart swelled. "Enjoy, gentlemen."

Dane cut into his steak, forked a piece and stuck it in his mouth. He chewed and groaned. "That's got to be the best steak I ever tasted."

A line of customers formed at the door. Victoria nodded in their direction and then smiled at Dane. "I'll leave you to your dinner. If there is anything else you need, please call out to me. I must seat my other customers, and then I'll be in the kitchen."

Thirty minutes later, Victoria returned to the Cholua brothers' table with a pot of coffee and three china cups and saucers. She sat next to the older brother and poured the coffee. "I believe the last time we met, Dane, I told you I'd like to speak with you about something." She passed him his coffee. "I hope you don't mind if I call you Dane."

The older brother shrugged. "That's my name." He accepted the cup and saucer. "What was it you wanted to talk about—Victoria?"

She handed Jake his coffee. Without taking even a sip of the hot beverage, he looked toward the staircase. "Did you tell Ruby I'm down here?"

Victoria brought both hands to her cheeks. "I'm so sorry, Jake. I've been so busy, I haven't had a chance to speak with her. I believe I heard her on the stairs a little while ago. Several men came in through the back entrance shortly after you arrived and went into the gaming room, so I would imagine by now things are getting rather interesting." She pointed to an open hallway toward the rear of the restaurant. "Go down that way and knock on the door."

Jake hurried to where she pointed. Victoria returned her attention to Dane. "I understand you knew Ben Rumson."

Dane's eyes opened wide. "Well—yeah—not exactly—we sorta knew him. Actually, it's kind of a funny story."

She gazed around the room, assuring herself that her other customers were enjoying their meals, and then returned her attention to Dane. "I'm always intrigued by funny stories. Certainly, I would like to hear one that involved Mr. Rumson. My experience with the man was never one I would refer to as funny. However, please tell me your tale."

"Well . . . one day a few months back, I found Ben lying along the creek. I checked him out, and thinkin' he was dead, I started diggin' a hole to bury him."

Victoria gasped.

Dane continued. "Well, shortly after that, Big John and Jake got there and Rumson started movin'." He slapped his leg. "I tell you . . . I never in all my days was so slack jawed."

Victoria held her hand to her chest. "Well, I'm sure Mr. Rumson was most appreciative that you had not buried him alive."

Dane shrugged. "Yeah, he thanked me for not buryin' him and all, but . . ."

"Yes?"

"Well even back then—I had this gut feelin'—I just didn't trust the man."

"I'd say you're a fine judge of character, Dane." She laid her hand on his. "Did you believe him to be—how can I politely say this? Did you think he might be of less than reputable character?"

Dane hung his head and lowered his voice. "He stole our claim. I found gold in the hole I was diggin', and the next day Rumson beat me to the recorder's office and claimed it was his."

Victoria laid both hands on the table. "No!" She burst into laughter.

Dane's eyes narrowed and he worked his jaw.

"I am sorry. You must forgive me." Victoria said. "It's just that this afternoon I went to the recorder's office and made claim to that piece of ground. As it had not been worked for so long, it was available to anyone wanting it."

CHAPTER

3

Mid-October 1860
Hole in the Ground Mining Claim
On a mountainside near Missouri Lake

A month had passed since Dane stormed out of The Towering Pines. The thought that Victoria Cashman owned his claim still caused him to fume, and Jake taking up with Ruby was another problem entirely.

Dane and Big John were finishing construction on a cabin, so between working in the mine and building their new home, he had little extra time for thinking about anything else. However, sitting alone in camp, Dane's thoughts returned to Victoria, Ruby, and his younger brother. Beneath a bright morning sun, he grumbled as he ate his squirrel hash breakfast. A large shadow appeared in front of him, and a gruff voice came from behind. "You're lookin' awful down in the mouth for a feller who found a handful of nuggets yesterday."

Dane turned. "Where you been? When you didn't come back last night, I got a little worried."

The blacksmith poured a cup of coffee. "Had some work that needed takin' care of."

"Thought Timmy was pretty much runnin' things down there."

"Yeah and he's doin' a fine job. But, he ain't quite strong enough to handle the smithy work. Had a couple folks needin' their horses shod."

Dane tossed coffee grounds from the bottom of his cup into the fire and headed for the cabin. "Don't suppose you saw Jake around."

Big John cleared his throat. "Uhmm—yeah—didn't see him."

"But—?"

"Might be you oughta get yourself into town and check things out."

Dane spun on his heel and pushed his wide-brimmed, brown hat back from his forehead. "Why? What's he up to?"

"Not too sure; but, I'm thinkin' he might be in over his head with Miss Ruby. Heard rumors Jake's gettin' himself quite a reputation up at The Tollgate."

Dane jerked his head to one side. "Yeah?"

"Yeah. Folks are sayin'—now mind you I'm just tellin' you the gossip. Folks are sayin' Jake's . . . well, I heard a feller say that Jake leads the lambs to slaughter and Miss Ruby fleeces 'em."

Without another word, Dane grabbed his jacket and headed west.

Big John shouted after him. "Hey, town's the other way. Know you ain't been there in awhile; but, figured you knew how to get there."

Dane muttered under his breath and kept walking. Jake was a grown man. He could make his own decisions—even if they were stupid decisions.

Big John caught up to Dane. "You goin' to the mine?"

"I need to bust me some rock!"

"Well you ain't goin' in there alone. I'm goin' with you."

"Suit yourself. I'm not very good company right now."

The big man chuckled. "Never would of guessed."

As they entered the underground chasm, Dane grabbed a lantern from one of the side timbers and lit it. "Don't know what Jake was thinkin' throwin' in with that woman?"

Big John lit his own lantern. "You think he's comin' back?"

"Guess he'll be back when he needs somethin' he ain't got down there."

The blacksmith laughed. "And what might he find up here he ain't gettin' down there?"

Dane shrugged. His friend was right. What could Jake get from the Hole in the Ground he could not get in town working with Ruby and fleecing their hardworking friends? They reached the entrance to a shaft, and John led the way down the ladder. Dane sighed. "Jake ain't got no sense when it comes to pretty women, and he enjoys a good time more than most. I figure when he gets tired of hangin' onto her petticoats, and realizes how low he's stooped, he'll be back."

An hour later, a familiar voice echoed down the tunnel, "Dane? Big John?"

Dane shouted, "Down here."

The younger brother appeared at the entrance to the shaft. "Guess you're mad at me, huh?"

Dane pounded his pick against the rock wall. "Nope."

"Sorry if I worried you."

"Figured you'd be back when you were ready."

"Ah, darn it, Dane. I done did it again."

Dane wanted to laugh, but remained stoic. "She send you away, or did you leave on your own?"

"Can't we just forget about it? I'm back. That's all there is to it."

Big John pounded his chisel against rock. "Get yourself back to camp, grab a pick and shovel, and get back to work."

"You been spendin' way too much time 'round Dane." Jake shouted back. "You're gettin' bossy as he is."

Dane swung his pick hard against the granite wall. The vein grew wider as they went further down. The deeper they went, the more difficult it became to work the gold out of the hard rock. Placer mining did not get them as much as they had found since they started in the mine, but working the creek wasn't near as backbreaking work.

Jake returned to the shaft and started down the ladder. As he stepped closer to Dane, he said, "Did you know Miss Ruby carried a pistol?"

CHAPTER

Meanwhile Back in Town—

Victoria's gaze went to an upstairs window in The Tollgate Saloon. A young, blonde woman, clothed in a corset and sheer wrap shouted, "No ladies allowed."

Straightening her blue linen jacket over her crisp, white blouse and then smoothing the front of her grey, wool skirt, Victoria arched an eyebrow. "I'm sorry. Aren't you a lady?"

The girl slapped her hand on the windowsill and tossed her head back. "I've been called a lot of things; but, a lady has never been one of them."

An older woman, wearing a light blue dress, her hair piled atop her head, pulled the younger one from the window and slammed the glass pane down.

The front door to The Tollgate opened, and a scowling man dressed in a white apron stood in the entry. "Can I help you?"

Victoria chuckled. "Do you greet all of your customers in such a friendly manner?"

The man sighed. "I'm sorry ma'am. We don't allow ladies in The Tollgate."

"Yes, I heard. However, I am not here to socialize. I am looking for my sister."

He rolled his eyes. "Like I said, ma'am. There ain't any ladies here."

She pointed, directing her gaze to the window upstairs. "What do you call them?"

"They ain't no ladies. That's for certain." He crooked his head to one side. "You thinkin' your sister's one of them gals up there?"

"No. I'm certain she isn't upstairs. She might be in your back room entertaining your customers with a game of Faro."

His eyes grew wide. "Oh, you mean Miss Ruby." He scanned Victoria from head to toe and shook his head. "I heard tell she had a sister. Heard she owned the new restaurant up yonder. That be you?"

She nodded. "Yes. That would be me. So, is my sister here?"

"No ma'am. Miss Ruby's games don't start till late in the evenin'." He rubbed his clean-shaven chin, his eyes narrowing. "Don't know where she'd be this time of day."

Victoria extended a gloved hand. "I thank you for your time, sir. If you should see her, please tell her I am looking for her."

The man shook her hand. "Yes ma'am. I'll do that. Hope she's alright."

Withdrawing her hand, Victoria's heartbeat quickened. "Is there any reason she wouldn't be?"

"Well, after that shootin' last night, folks were talkin' how you don't mess with the Bummer's Gang or they'll come lookin' for you. That feller's shoulder was bleedin' somethin' awful when they took him outta here."

The small knot that had resided in her stomach since the night before tightened. Her breathing grew labored, heat rose into her face, and her legs weakened. "Shooting?"

The man in the doorway hurried down the steps and put an arm beneath Victoria's. "I'm thinkin' you'd best sit a spell, ma'am. You're lookin' kind of poorly."

She nodded. "If I could just come inside . . . ."

The man escorted Victoria through the door and lowered her onto the closest chair. He slid in behind the bar. "I'll get you a glass of water. You want me to send someone for the doc?"

"I don't believe I need a doctor. But, a glass of water would be nice. Please tell me more about the shooting. How was Ruby involved?"

He handed her the drink and sat in a chair facing her. "You sure you're gonna be alright?"

She forced her breathing to slow and took small sips of the cool liquid. "Just tell me what happened."

A tall man, wearing a broad brimmed, dark hat, and a holstered pistol on his hip, entered through the front door.

The bartender's body grew tense and his lips formed a tight line. He whispered, "I'll be right back, just let me take care of this customer." As he stood behind the bar, he inhaled and then exhaled a deep breath. "What can I get you?"

The stranger eyed Victoria with a smirk and a raised eyebrow. "I'll take one of those, Sam."

The bartender shook his head and stammered, "She—don't—she don't work here."

The man smacked his lips as he held a dark icy stare on Victoria. "Too bad. I'd pay a pound of gold for time with her."

Victoria stood, bracing herself on the table with one hand. "I'm feeling better now. Maybe I'll stop back later, and we can finish our discussion—Sam."

The stranger swaggered toward the staircase at the far end of the room and ascended several steps before looking back. "Don't worry yourself, missy. I ain't gonna bother you. I'll take my money where it's appreciated. You and Sam here can continue with whatever you was talkin' about."

Sam returned to sit with Victoria. "I'm real sorry about that, ma'am."

Victoria lowered herself onto her chair. "Who was that?"

"Name's Coleman. Heard tell he lives up in the hills somewhere. Mean sort of feller."

"You said someone was shot last night." Victoria said. "Was my sister hurt?"

"No ma'am. It was her that done the shootin.'"

She closed her eyes. "Not again."

"You mean she's done it before?"

"Last time was in Wichita. She said he pulled his gun first, but I'm not so sure. Ruby's got quite a temper, and nothing gets her stirred up as much as someone cheating at cards."

"She ever kill anybody?"

Victoria shook her head. "No. Thank heavens. She's lucky she hasn't been shot or hung."

Sam laughed. "Oh, ma'am, there ain't nobody would hang Miss Ruby. She's too dang pretty to get lynched."

"Who did she shoot?"

"Feller they call Chuck-a-luck. I heard tell he skedaddled up here from Denver after the Turkey War—one of the Bummer's Gang they didn't catch and lynch."

"Do you know why she shot him?"

"Not real sure. They were shoutin' somethin' about Ben Rumson. Next thing I knew, Jake Cholua came runnin' out sayin' Miss Ruby had a pistol, and somebody needed to stop her before she hurt herself or anybody else." His eyes grew wide. "It was right after that she shot ole Chuck-a-luck. I heard the *bang!* Then everything got quiet."

Victoria's mouth went dry. "So what happened to Ruby?"

Sam shook his head. "Don't know. I sent for the doc and went back to tend to Chuck-a-luck." He shrugged. "When I came out, she and Jake were both gone."

"Could she be with Jake?"

"Can't say for sure. Jake's been stayin' at Miss Maggies. You might check there."

Victoria stood, swallowed a long gulp of water, and headed for the door as Sam shouted after her. "Sure hope Miss Ruby's alright."

As she ran from The Tollgate toward Miss Maggie's boarding house, she passed Timmy standing in front of the blacksmith shop. He shouted after her, "Where you headed in such a hurry, Miss Vicki?"

Victoria brushed falling hair from her face and worked to adjust the pins that came loose during her race up the hill. "I'm looking for Ruby. Have you seen her?"

"No ma'am."

"Have you seen Jake Cholua?"

Timmy nodded and grinned. "Yes, ma'am. I just saw him this mornin'."

Victoria's gaze went to the sign on the front of the boarding house. "Did he go into Miss Maggie's?"

He shook his head. "Oh, no ma'am. He said he was headin' up to . . . uhh . . . I mean he said he was goin' fishin'."

The hesitancy in the boy's reply raised Victoria's suspicions. "Is there something you're not telling me?"

"No ma'am."

She placed her hands on her hips and narrowed her eyes. "Timmy, are you forgetting your mother works for me? Do I need to go get her to find out what is going on?"

He lowered his gaze and shuffled his boot across the loose ground, sending straw and stones scattering. "No ma'am."

She placed her hand beneath his chin, raised his face, and looked into his eyes. "It is very important that I find Jake Cholua. Do you know where he is?"

Timmy stepped back a few paces, keeping his eyes lowered, hands in his pants pockets. "Mr. John made me promise not to tell anybody where they were. I'm always supposed to say they went fishin'."

"Well, Timmy, I wouldn't want you to break a promise, however, I'm very worried about my sister, Ruby. I thought she might be with Jake."

The boy shook his head. "Oh, no ma'am—She weren't with Jake."

Victoria's gaze went toward the mountains beyond Black Hawk Pointe. "Do you know how to get to where John Schmidt and the Cholua brothers have their claim?"

Timmy's eyes grew wide. "How'd you know 'bout their claim?"

She shrugged. "Let's just say I don't miss much, and people tend to talk when they're enjoying a good meal." She placed her hands on her hips and leaned down eye-to-eye with the young man. "So where is it?"

"I ain't never been there." He walked into the middle of Gregory Street and pointed northeast. "It's up that way someplace near Missouri Lake. That's all I know."

She patted his cheek. "Thank you so much, Timmy." She started toward home, stopped mid pace, turned around, and shouted back to the boy, "If you see Ruby, tell her to come to The Towering Pines—and tell her if I'm not there to wait for me to return."

CHAPTER

After leaving Timmy at the livery, Victoria was determined to ride out and look for her sister. Several weeks earlier, in anticipation of working Rumson's claim, she purchased an assortment of men's clothing. Assuming the ride up the mountain would be rugged, and hoping to dissuade anyone from recognizing her as a woman, and possibly accosting her, she pulled the blue jeans over her bloomers. Buttoning the chambray shirt, she then stuffed the bottom half into her pants. She tugged the heavy work boots over two pairs of stockings and pulled on a grey felt hat. She admired her reflection in the mirror. In spite of her anxiety over her sister's disappearance, a smile of satisfaction tugged at the corners of her lips. "That should do it."

In a small enclosure behind the restaurant, she saddled and mounted her chestnut mare then cantered down Gregory Street to Clear Creek. She followed the trail along the creek's banks for about a mile to where the path became steep and rocky. She continued up the mountainside. When the course became too rugged, she dismounted and led her horse until the grade leveled out. Ahead she spotted the shimmering waters of what she assumed was Missouri Lake. There were no signs of a campsite or mining claim. Her heart plummeted in disappointment. "Now where to?" A twig snapped in the wooded thicket. She grabbed her rifle from behind her saddle and turned.

A large man, carrying two dead rabbits in one hand and a rifle in the other, stood before her. "Where you headed, young feller?"

She exhaled as she looked into friendly hazel eyes set in a boyish face.

His lips twisted into a half grin. "Excuse me ma'am. Guess you ain't no feller."

Victoria bit at her bottom lip and then shook her head. "What gave me away?"

He tilted his head to one side, and then the other, looking her over. "Well, I ain't never seen no feller with a face pretty as yours or—filled out like you."

Her cheeks grew warm. "Oh!"

"What's a lady like you doin' up here? Ain't safe you know." His gaze went to the rock cliff above and then down the trail from where she came. "Injuns. Mountain lions. Bears . . . and a lot of ornery two legged critters who'd just a soon shoot you as look at you."

Victoria swallowed hard. "Really?"

"So, what you doin' up here?"

"I'm looking for my sister."

The big man laughed. "Well, I ain't seen no ladies in these parts, and we've been up here a good long while." He scratched his head. "What made you think you'd find her this far from town?"

"Last she was seen, she was with a man by the name of Jake Cholua. I heard he and his brother were mining up here, and I was hoping to find him—and maybe her."

The man's eyes opened wide and his smile broadened. "You don't say. Jake, huh?"

"Do you know him?" She searched the surrounding landscape. "Have you seen him?"

He took the reins of her horse in hand. "Sure enough have. Come with me. I'll take you to him."

She grabbed the reins back. "Sir, you are most kind and seem like an honest man. However, if you think I'm going to trust a complete stranger and go off with you, you are sadly mistaken."

The man lay the rabbits on the ground and then lay his rifle next to them. He removed his tattered hat and bowed. "John Schmidt at your service, ma'am. Folks call me Big John." He grinned. "And I'm thinkin' you might be Victoria Cashman, owner of The Towering Pines and sister of Miss Ruby Cashman."

Her mouth formed an O as she gripped Big John's arm. "You're John Schmidt? Praise God! Where's Jake? Have you seen Ruby? Did you hear about the shooting? Do you know if Ruby is alright?"

John took her hands in his. "Calm down. Yes, I'm John Schmidt. Don't know what God thinks 'bout me—but, I try. Last I saw Jake, he was cleanin' up over at our campsite. He told me 'bout a shootin' last night. But, I don't know where Miss Ruby might be. She was fine last Jake saw her. Now, you comin' with me, or not?"

She nodded and followed the big man across the wide expanse of open land and into a wooded area. A hammer pounding nails echoed through the stillness and the smell of smoke lingered in the air.

As they approached the campsite, Victoria's heart leapt at the sight of Dane Cholua. It had been weeks since she had laughed at him and his story about Ben Rumson. So many times, she recounted that scene, and so many times she regretted her reaction. The object of her distracted thoughts hammered a shingle into the rooftop of a small cabin. She shook her head. She wasn't there to see Dane. She had to find Ruby.

After Big John pegged her horse in a patch of grass, the two walked side by side toward the cabin. Jake stoked the campfire with more wood and then turned to face them, his eyes growing wide. "Miss Cashman? What in tarnation are you doin' up here, and what you doin' in them clothes?"

Dane climbed down a ladder from the rooftop, and with a half smile on his lips, he locked a blue-eyed stare on Victoria. He shook his head. "You do look—well, you sure don't look like you did the last time I saw you."

She glared at Jake. "Do you know where Ruby is?"

"I ain't seen her since last night." He stomped and grabbed his head with both hands. "No! I knew I shouldn't of left her run off by herself. I just knew it."

Victoria gripped Jake by the shoulders, digging in her fingers. Her heartbeat pulsed in her head. "Jake, stop it. What do you mean? Where is she?"

The man wrenched himself free of her grasp. "I don't know."

Victoria forced back tears. "No one has seen her since she left The Tollgate. Sam said the last time he saw her she was with you."

Jake sat on a log by the fire. "We thought it best if we got outta there. Someone said the feller she shot was one of the Bummer's Gang. The other three were part of the gang, too. We didn't know what they might do."

Dane stood behind his brother and laid a hand on his shoulder. "Just tell us what happened."

Victoria sat next to Jake, her hands folded on her knees. In spite of her soft undergarments, the rough fabric of her clothing chaffed her skin, and she had rubbed blisters on her heals from the boots.

Jake removed his hat and dropped his gaze. "Ruby was playin' cards with three fellers. One went by the name of Bill, the other Tom, and then there was the feller she shot. They called him Chuck-a-luck. Well, he was losin' bad all night, and the more he lost the madder he got. He kept blamin' Ruby for

24

him losin'. But, I swear she weren't cheatin'. She's one good card player. She kept watchin' Chuck-a-luck. One time when she got up from the table between games, she whispered to me that she was sure he was cheatin'. But, he still weren't winnin'."

Jake looked at Victoria. "Ruby hates cheaters. But, since the feller kept losin' she was alright with it. Then Chuck-a-luck asks Ruby if she knew a feller named Rumson. He said Ben Rumson was the best card player he'd ever seen, and he was pretty sure Rumson could even beat Ruby."

Jake's eyes grew wide. "Now that got her riled, and they started arguing about Ben Rumson. Ruby said he was a cheat and a liar who deserved what he got. Chuck-a-luck laughed and said if she kept cheatin' him she might end up the same way."

Victoria gasped. "Do you think that man killed Ruby?"

Jake shook his head. "Naw. She winged him good. Don't think he'll be shootin' anyone anytime soon."

Big John put the rabbits on a spit over the campfire and looked at Jake. "So why did she shoot him?"

"I ain't too sure 'cause everything happened so fast. Ruby stood up shoutin' at Chuck-a-luck, tellin' him she ran the table and it was time for him to leave. He put his hand inside his jacket. Next I know, Ruby pulls a pistol out of her skirt and shoots him."

"You think she meant to kill him?" Dane asked.

"No." Victoria answered. "If she meant to kill him, he'd be dead."

CHAPTER

Victoria's stomach growled as Big John passed metal plates to her, Dane, and Jake. "Dinner's ready." He said. After ladling several scoops of beans onto his plate, he ripped a sizable chunk of meat from one of the rabbits. "Get it while it's hot!"

"I guess I could eat before I go." She said.

Big John helped her to her feet. "You ain't goin' nowhere by yourself, missy."

"You're coming with me?"

"You don't think we'd let you go off alone, do you? Who knows what kind of trouble you might get into?" He winked and then filled her plate. "You get your belly full, and get a good night's sleep, and we'll head out at first light."

A tear slipped down her cheek and she brushed it away. "I don't even know where to look for her."

Jake kicked an escaping branch back into the fire. "Last I saw her she was headed up Gregory Street." He shook his head. "I knew I should have walked with her. But, she said I should go on to Miss Maggie's and she'd see me tonight at The Tollgate."

Victoria wiped her nose on her shirtsleeve and brushed away tears. "Do you think those men might have done something to her?"

"I'm pretty sure the other two went up to Doc Reed's with Chuck-a-luck." Jake rubbed his chin. "There was another feller came by earlier in the evenin'. He didn't say much. Just smiled and tipped his hat to Miss Ruby, then he gave the fellers playin' cards an ugly look, like he weren't none too happy with 'em. After he left, Bill said somethin' about getting sick and tired of him bossin' 'em around."

"Did you get his name?" Victoria asked.

"They never did say. But, Sam said somethin' about Coleman bein' right mad 'cause the other three were playin' cards with Miss Ruby. He said Coleman had his sights set on her from the first time he saw her." Jake scrunched his lips and furrowed his brow. "I told Sam to tell that Coleman feller Miss Ruby was with me, and he'd best be movin' on."

A knot formed in Victoria's throat. "I met him."

"When?" Dane said.

"This afternoon—at The Tollgate. Sam said Coleman lives in the hills around here somewhere, and he's one mean fellow." She hugged herself and shuddered. "The way he leered at me when Sam told him I wasn't one of the girls made me sick."

Dane looked at Big John. "You ever hear of him?"

The blacksmith nodded. "Sure 'nough have. From what I hear tell, he was one of the Bummers. He and the other three showed up in town a couple days ago. Seems after the folks in Dener went to lynchin' the rest of them, they're the only ones left."

For several moments, no one spoke. Victoria's mind whirled, and she gripped Dane's hand. Her thoughts escaped in a whisper. "What if they have Ruby?'

Dane shook his head. "Don't go thinkin' like that."

A tear slipped down her cheek. "It's the only thing that makes any sense. Why wouldn't she come back to The Towering Pines? Where else would she go?"

"You said you saw this Coleman feller at The Tollgate this afternoon, right?"

Victoria nodded.

"So, if he was in town . . . ."

"Yeah, if he was in town," Jake interrupted. "He couldn't have Ruby."

"We need to find out where the other three were today and where they're hiding out," Dane said.

As they finished their meal, the sun hung low on the western horizon and Dane stood. "It's gonna be dark soon. Let's get some sleep and we'll head into town in the mornin' and find out where Coleman and his friends might be." He offered his hand to Victoria. "You can sleep in the cabin, and we'll sleep out here."

With Dane's assistance, Victoria pulled herself up and faced him. "Thank you. However, I doubt I'll sleep a wink with worrying about Ruby."

CHAPTER

7

Several hours later, the campfire waned to near embers and the impending darkness moved in like a devouring void. Victoria regretted not thinking to ask for a lantern when she went to bed. With fading coals lighting her way, she tiptoed out of the cabin and toward a cluster of bushes. As she passed by the three men, Big John snorted. She stepped on a twig that snapped with a loud *crack!* Dane was on his feet in less than a second, his Winchester pointed straight at her. He lowered the barrel. "Good gracious, woman. You gave me a start. What you doin' traipsin' around this hour of the night?"

Her face grew warm as she held up a handful of newsprint and shrugged. "I need to . . . ."

"Oh!" Dane came closer to where she could make out his features. "Sorry. You go on over there." He pointed in the direction she was headed. "I'll wait till you get back in the cabin—if that's okay with you." The whites of his eyes shone bright from the flickering embers. "I mean . . . Oh shucks!"

She laid her hand on his arm. "I'd be more comfortable if you'd just lay back down and ignore me, please." She inhaled a deep breath and then exhaled. "I'm sure I'll be fine—over there—by myself."

Dane tossed more wood on the fire, and it erupted into a roaring flame, lighting the entire campsite. "I'll be right here—sleepin'." He laid his rifle next to his bedroll and slipped between the blankets. "You just go on now."

From her hidden spot in the shrubbery, Victoria watched the flames dance and leap. She looked away only long enough to redress.

Hoof beats broke the peaceful silence of the night. The incoming visitors shouted vulgarities and one rider tossed what looked like a body to the ground. It landed with a thud and Victoria thought she heard a muffled cry. She buttoned her pants, and peeked through the shrubbery. Coleman and three others—she assumed to be Bill, Tom, and Chuck-a-luck—sat astride their horses. Whomever they had thrown to the ground groaned and muttered something undistinguishable. Victoria stifled a gasp as she recognized the voice as Ruby's. Her instincts shouted at her to run to her sister's aid. With all the self-control she could muster, she remained in the bushes.

Jake hurried to Ruby's side and helped her to her feet. "Ruby? Darlin' you alright?" He raised his eyes toward Coleman. "What did you do to her?"

Coleman scoffed. "She's okay—Just knocked her around a bit. She's lucky I didn't shoot her after what she done to Chuck-a-luck."

The man with the strange name sat in his saddle, his right arm in a sling.

Coleman scanned the campsite. "She's more trouble than she's worth." He ran a hand across his whiskered chin. "Hear tell you fellers got a claim up here." He cocked his pistol and pointed it at Dane. "So we figured you must have a stash of gold, and we're gonna take it off your hands."

Dane's Winchester lay next to his bedroll. He took several steps backwards. "You heard wrong mister. We're just up here fishin'." Stepping further into the shadows, he opened his arms wide. "You see any minin' gear round here?"

The man to the far left sneered. "The boy at the livery told us you fellers been bringin' gold outta here for the past couple of months."

Coleman turned his head with a sharp move. "Shut-up, Bill."

In two long strides, Big John reached Coleman, yanked him from his horse, and threw him to the ground. Coleman's pistol fired as he landed, the bullet narrowly missing the blacksmith's head. After kicking the outlaw's firearm to the side, John grabbed him up by the front of his shirt. "If you hurt Timmy, so help me, I'll kill you."

Dane grabbed his rifle and pointed it toward Coleman's cohorts. "I'd suggest you gentlemen get off those horses and step on down here, hands in the air."

While John and Dane distracted the outlaws, Victoria slipped into the cabin and collected her rifle. Now standing in the open doorway, she fired a shot at the ground beneath Bill, Tom, and Chuck-a-luck's horses, sending the animals rearing and the riders plummeting to the ground. "You heard the man." Victoria said, "What are you waiting for?"

Big John held Coleman's hands behind his back. "Miss Cashman, there's rope in the cabin. Could you bring it to me? I'm thinkin' the law might be lookin' for these fellers. Maybe even got a bounty on 'em."

While Dane collected the men's guns, Victoria retrieved the rope and took a length to Big John. Then she took the rest to Dane, keeping her rifle trained on the other three while he tied them up.

As John tied Coleman to a tree, he pulled extra tight on the rope and yanked the man's head back by his hair. "What did you do to Timmy?"

Coleman snorted. "Ahh! We just scared him a little. Amazing how much you can get a kid to talk when you hold him over a fire."

Big John swung his mighty fist, landing squarely on Coleman's jaw and knocking the man out cold. The blacksmith collected one of the outlaw's horses and mounted. "I gotta get to town and check on Timmy."

As John disappeared into the darkness, Victoria helped Dane tie the men's feet. While he dragged them further into the woods, she rounded up the other three horses and pegged them near her mare. She returned to the campsite and swiped her hands against one another. "Don't think they'll be goin' anywhere for awhile."

On the far side of the campfire, Ruby sat with Jake, the younger sister's voice a welcome sound to Victoria's ears. "Jake, please quit fussing. I'll be fine." Ruby limped toward the campfire and warmed her hands. She winked at Victoria. "I've taken worse—and you know it."

CHAPTER

J ake wrapped an arm around Ruby and lowered her to a
log next to the fire. "I'm thinkin' there's more to you ladies
than just a pretty face." He raised his eyes to Victoria. "You
mind tellin' us how it is you and Ruby knew how to handle the
likes of them fellers?"

Victoria chuckled as she seated herself next to Dane. "It's
a long story, Jake. Growing up with a sheriff for your dad and
four older brothers—Well, if we didn't learn how to take care
of ourselves, they would have kept us in tears most of our
childhood."

Dane poked at the fire with a stick. "I'm thinkin' it ain't
no coincidence you two showed up in town right behind Ben
Rumson and right before the Bummers gang."

Ruby rolled her eyes. "We heard rumors in Wichita that
Rumson was here in Black Hawk Pointe, so we followed him."
She rubbed her hip and then placed her hands in the small of
her back. "Victoria was running a hotel over there. One day
early last spring, Ben came in dressed in his fine suit, wearing
a beaver-skin top hat. He smooth talked both us."

Victoria nodded. "After all the wild cowboys and traveling
salesmen, it was nice to see someone so refined and educated."

"He did wear fine clothes and talked like a gentleman," Dane said. "Other than gettin' drunk and passin' out along the road, I guess our first impression was he was an okay sort of feller." He chuckled. "But, we've all had our moments of stupid."

Victoria hung her head. "He courted me for over two months. He was always bringing me a new dress or hat or pieces of fine jewelry, and he even asked me to marry him."

Dane raised his head with a jerk. "He what?"

She sighed. "Yes. I hate to admit it. I fell in love with the man."

"You weren't the only one he fooled," Ruby said. "He was always sending rich men to my card games. When he played, he'd win and lose like a gentleman—though he did win more than he lost."

Jake shrugged. "So what happened?"

Victoria brushed a lock of hair from her face. "One morning, I came down to the front desk, and the safe door was standing open. All the money was gone—and as I soon learned, so was Ben. I went up to his room to tell him I'd been robbed, and found he and all his belongings had vanished."

Ruby sat next to Jake. "The night before, we had the biggest game I've ever sat in. Thousands of dollars at stake—and I won." She winced and then exhaled. "When the game was over, Ben walked me back to the hotel. He offered to put the money in the safe for me. He knew the combination, because he took our deposits to the bank for us. I had no reason not to trust him."

Jake scratched his head. "That first night we met, you said he only owed you a couple hundred dollars. You never said he'd done all that."

Ruby nodded. "Back then, I didn't know who I could trust. I figured if I wanted to get our money back I needed to cozy up to Ben. So, I flirted with him and acted like the money didn't matter that much."

Victoria tossed a log on the fire. "By the time I got to Black Hawk Pointe, Ben was dead."

A voice echoed from the forest. "Hey! You can't leave us like this."

Dane stood and disappeared into the wooded thicket. Several moments later, he reappeared wearing a smirk. "That should shut 'em up."

Victoria stretched her feet toward the fire. "What did you do?"

"I gagged 'em with their kerchiefs."

To the east, the sky's opalescent hue announced the dawning of a new day.

Jake crooked his head toward the trees. "We takin' them to town this mornin'?"

Dane scrunched his lips as though deep in thought. "I'm thinkin' you ought to go get the sheriff and some men. We ain't gonna try to take all four of 'em down this mountain by ourselves."

Jake stood and kissed Ruby on the top of the head. "Guess you're in good hands here."

She smiled and nodded.

Dane helped Victoria to her feet and looked at his younger brother. "Check on Timmy and Big John while you're down there."

Victoria bit at her bottom lip. "I hope they didn't hurt that boy. He's such a sweet child. I'm sure he didn't willingly tell them where we were, and his mother doesn't need any more grief in her life. Angie's had more than enough with losing her husband so young."

CHAPTER

Black Hawk Pointe

J ake rode up Gregory Street at a full run and reined the horse in front of the livery. He called out, "Big John? Timmy?" After searching the forge and stalls and not finding the blacksmith or his young friend, he hurried across the street to The Towering Pines.

Angie set a hot skillet away from the flame as Jake walked into the kitchen. Fatigue settled in the pockets beneath her normally sparkling blue eyes.

He plunked into a chair. "Timmy and John here?"

The mother pointed upstairs. "Mr. Schmidt put Timmy to bed as soon as they got here." Her words sounded as hollow as she looked, and she pushed several strands of blonde hair back from her face. "I feel terrible that I didn't check on him when he didn't show up at the usual time. We were so busy last night—and with Victoria gone . . . ."

Jake shrugged. "I guess John told you what happened?"

"He did. I'm certainly relieved Victoria and Ruby are alright."

"And, Timmy?"

"He'll be fine. Other than a few scratches and some scorched spots on his britches, he's no worse for what happened." She clenched her fists. "I'd just like to get my hands on those hooligans that did that to him."

Jake choked back a chuckle at the thought of the petite woman going up against Coleman and his friends. "I came to town to get the sheriff. Right now, they're tied up good and tight."

She exhaled. "Good!"

Jake reached the top of the stairs and found the door to Timmy's room standing open. Big John sat on a chair next to the boy's bed. The blacksmith whispered, "He's finally sleepin'."

Jake motioned for John to follow him into the hall. "What did they do to him?"

John clenched his jaw. "Timmy said they came in askin' if he knew where you were. They didn't believe him when he told them he didn't know." John grinned. "He's not a very good liar."

"Coleman said they held him over a fire. What exactly happened?"

John frowned. "Timmy said they fired up the forge, and two of them held him just above the flames to get him to talk."

"Did he get burned?"

"No. Thank God. His pants got a little burnt. But, he's okay. When I got to town, I went straight to the livery and found him curled up in the corner of a stall. Poor little guy. I tried to pick him up. He pushed me away and said he was alright and he was real sorry he told them fellers where our claim was."

Jake shook his head and pounded a fist into his opposite palm. "I'd love to hold them over the fire. I'd burn more than their britches."

John glanced back into the room. "I'm gonna stay with him until Miss Angie closes up. I'll probably bunk over at Miss Maggie's." He furrowed his brow. "You fellas and the ladies gonna be alright?"

"Yeah. Dane, Miss Ruby, and Miss Victoria are up at the campsite. I came into town to get the sheriff and some men to collect Coleman and his buddies."

John returned to Timmy's bedside. "I'll see you sometime tomorrow."

Jake nodded and hurried down the stairs. He tipped his hat to Angie. "Looks like he's gonna be fine."

She smiled. "Praise God."

As Jake rode up Gregory Street toward Central City, a young couple came walking down the hill. The woman carried a crying baby and tear trails streaked her dusty cheeks. They were new faces in town and something about the scene broke Jake's heart. Many people came looking for gold and ended up with no money and no place to go. Something else seemed amiss. "You folks need some help?"

The man raised his eyes. "Don't know if there's much of anything you can do, mister. Thanks for askin'."

Jake dismounted. "Where you headed?"

"We were on our way to Russell's Gulch to my wife's brother's place." The man said. "Yesterday, four men stopped us along the road and robbed us of pretty much everything."

"What did they look like?"

The man clenched his fists as he described the thieves. "They wore kerchiefs over their faces, so we didn't get a good look at them."

The woman raised watery blue eyes beneath a faded flowery sunbonnet and sniffed. "The one man got real mad at one of the others and swore at him. It seemed a strange name for a grown man. I thought he called him Chuck-a-luck."

A rekindled sense of vengeance raged inside Jake as he pointed toward The Towering Pines. He inhaled a deep breath to restrain his anger and then gripped the man's shoulder. "You go in there and tell Miss Angie that Jake sent you and I'll cover your meal."

The man shook Jake's hand. "That's mighty neighborly of you, mister. We'll pay you back just as soon as we can get to Russell's Gulch. Her brother owns a store up there. I'm sure he'll loan us the money."

"Don't worry about it." Jake started to mount his horse, but then turned back to the family entering the restaurant. "By the way, what's your name?"

The man shouted back. "I'm Clayton Cooper. This is my wife, Hannah, and our baby girl, Cassidy. We call her CC."

Jake tipped his hat. "I'm Jake Cholua, and I'm mighty glad to meet you folks."

When he reached the Sheriff's office in Central City, Jake stormed across the boardwalk and threw open the door. The single jail cell sat empty. A plate of half-eaten food and a partial cup of coffee sat on the sheriff's desk. Jake picked up the coffee cup. It was still warm. "Peck? You here?"

The back door swung open and Sheriff Peck entered. "Yeah, I'm here. What you want?"

"We got them outlaws tied up at our claim."

The sheriff sat down to finish his meal and drink his coffee. "No need to yell. I can hear you just fine. Now, what outlaws are you talkin' about?

"That Coleman feller and the other three." Jake paced the room, jabbing his right hand into his left palm. "They took Miss Ruby and beat her up somethin' awful. Then they came to our camp thinkin' they could steal our gold."

Sheriff Peck knocked over his chair, grabbed a rifle, and hurried toward the door. "Well, why didn't you say so? You show me where they are, and I'll take care of 'em."

"Don't you think you ought to get a few other fellers to help?"

"Who's watchin' 'em now?"

"Dane and Miss Victoria."

"Victoria Cashman?" The sheriff said. "Towering Pines Victoria?"

"Yes, sir."

The sheriff shook his head. "What about Ruby? She okay?"

Jake shrugged. "She said she's alright. But, she's pretty banged up."

"John Schmidt up there with you fellers?"

"Nope. He's over at the restaurant takin' care of Timmy."

The sheriff led the way out of his office and into the street, and the two men walked side by side to the livery while Jake filled the lawman in about what the outlaws did to Timmy and the Cooper family. "That's about it," Jake said. "Guess you heard about the shootin' at The Tollgate the other night."

"Yep. I heard," Sheriff Peck chuckled. "Sounds like Miss Ruby's got hidden talents."

"You ain't gonna arrest her—are you?"

"Nobody pressed no charges. And, the way I heard it—it was self-defense."

"So we gonna get some other fellers to help?"

Now inside the livery, the sheriff saddled and mounted his horse. "I'm thinkin' you, Dane, and I can handle 'em."

Jake scratched his head. "What if one of 'em makes a run for it?"

Sheriff Peck shrugged. "If they do—guess we'll just have to shoot 'em."

CHAPTER

Hole in the Ground Claim Site

As Jake road away, Victoria assisted Ruby into the cabin and then joined Dane at the campfire. "She gonna be alright," Dane asked.

Victoria nodded. "She's pretty tough."

Dane paced and sat on the ground beneath a large cottonwood tree. "Why don't you go back in the cabin and try to get some sleep. I'm gonna rest here until Jake gets back with the sheriff."

She sat next to him, pulling her legs to her chest. "If it's all the same to you, I'd rather rest here."

Dane's silent, deep blue gaze sent her heart racing.

She raised her chin and laid her hand on his arm. "Yes?"

"Nothing . . . it's just . . . ."

She drew in closer. Her body snuggled close to his. "Yes?"

He pulled his black hat over his eyes and laid his head against the tree. Moments later, his deep breathing indicated he had fallen asleep.

Victoria laid her head on his shoulder and sighed.

Hours later, bright yellow shafts of sunlight streamed between the overhead branches. Hoof-beats brought Dane to his feet, his rifle at ready.

"You can put that down," Jake shouted. "It's just me and Sheriff Peck."

"It's 'bout time you got back." Dane looked behind the two men. "Where's your posse?"

The sheriff dismounted and tipped his hat. "Afternoon, Miss Cashman." He grinned. "You are Miss Victoria Cashman, aren't you?"

Her cheeks grew warm as she brushed her hands across her chambray shirt and work pants. "Yes, it's me, Sheriff."

"Weren't certain seein' you in them clothes."

Dane interrupted the sheriff's teasing. "Where's the posse?"

Sheriff Peck tipped his hat again to Victoria, winked, and returned his attention to Dane. "After Jake told me how you took them fellers down by yourselves, didn't seem to me we needed any help." He glanced around the campsite. "Where are they?"

Victoria smiled sweetly at the sheriff and led the way into the woods. "They're back here." She kicked at Coleman's foot. "Keep a close eye on this one."

Dane followed behind. "And we'll be glad to be rid of 'em."

The outlaws struggled against their ropes and gags as the sheriff approached

Peck chuckled. "Yep! Looks like you got everything under control."

Victoria slipped her arm through the lawman's, more to taunt Dane than to encourage the sheriff. "I bet you're hungry after that long ride and climb up here. How about we settle down to a nice supper of rabbit stew before you head back?"

CHAPTER

Central City

Several hours later, as the sun sent ominous shadows yawning and stretching across Main Street, Victoria groaned. Her body ached from fatigue. She had scratched herself raw trying to stop the itch from the work clothes, and her feet were killing her.

Dane and Jake held their rifles pointed on the outlaws while Sheriff Peck walked the Bummer's gang into the jail cell. The sheriff unbound their hands. Immediately, Coleman yanked the kerchief from his mouth. "You can't treat us like this. We got rights, you know."

Peck slammed the cell door shut. "You can complain all you want to the marshal when he gets here in a few days. In the meantime, you'll get water, coffee, and three meals a day."

Dane and Jake slapped each other on the back and grinned as Victoria rolled her eyes.

"I'm glad that's over," she said. "I'm going to collect Ruby from Doc Taylor's office. I believe we've had enough excitement for today."

Sheriff Peck opened the door, allowing Victoria to walk out ahead of him. "Would you mind if I came with you to Doc Taylors? If she's up to it, I'd like to speak with Ruby about the location of the gang's hideout."

Victoria glanced back to confirm Dane was watching and then hooked her arm through Peck's. "I'm sure that will be fine, Sheriff."

Jake joined the two on the boardwalk. "I'm goin' down to check on the Coopers and make sure they got a place to stay tonight."

The sheriff stepped back inside his office. "You mind stayin' here until I get back, Dane?"

Dane's jaw tightened and he glared at the lawman. "No. That's just fine." He plunked into the chair behind the sheriff's desk and mumbled, "Yeah, that's—just—fine."

In Doc Taylor's office, Victoria helped Ruby into a cotton dress the doctor's wife had loaned her. "The sheriff wants to ask you some questions about the gang's hideout. Do you remember where it is?"

Ruby sighed as she tugged at the excess fabric at her sides. "Yes. I remember." She looked in a mirror and ran her hands through her tousled hair. "I don't suppose you have a scarf or something I can cover this mess with?"

Victoria handed her sister her gray felt hat and grinned. "Just this."

Ruby pulled the man's hat over her blonde curls, shoved her hair up inside, and looked in the mirror. "Oh, lovely!"

The sheriff called from the other side of the curtain, "You ladies decent?"

Ruby shook her head as she walked through the drape. "That's a matter of opinion." She started to laugh, but grabbed at her side as her breath caught. "Oh! That hurt."

The sheriff's eyes opened wide. "You sure you're up to talkin' with me?"

Ruby huffed. "Victoria says you want to know about the gang's hideout."

"You sure you're okay?"

"Yes—I'm fine." She slipped her arm through Victoria's, leaning on her sister for support. "They're in an old cabin in a place they called Four Mile Gulch. I recall riding through that area on the stagecoach when I came to Black Hawk Pointe. You can't see the cabin from the road. It's up a hill behind a rock outcropping."

The sheriff fingered the brim of his hat. "Anythin' else you remember?"

Ruby put her finger to her cheek and raised her eyes. "Yes. I remember a lone pine tree standing where we turned off the road. The ground is torn up pretty bad going up the hill toward those rocks."

Sheriff Peck offered Ruby a cushioned chair. "Anythin' inside of the cabin?"

Holding her side, Ruby sat. "The place was near to falling down. There was a large box of jewelry and a couple of silver tea services sitting on a bench." She closed her eyes and furrowed her brow. "There were clothes piled in one corner, and all sorts of cooking utensils, plates, and other stuff. When they left this morning, they put me in another building out behind the cabin. There were bags of feed, flour, sugar, and coffee beans."

The sheriff nodded. "Yeah, that sounds about right. From the reports I've gotten from folks in Black Hawk Pointe and Central City, those are the kind of things got stolen. Did you see any wagons or horses?"

"They had several wagons between the cabin and that building, and a corral that held several teams of horses and a couple of saddle horses."

The sheriff pulled up a chair and sat in front of Ruby. He patted her hand. "I hate to keep you any longer. You need to get some rest. But, is there anythin' else you can tell me?"

Her eyes filled with tears. "Only that those men deserve to hang for what they've done. They're evil, Sheriff. They're just plain evil."

Victoria laid her arm across her sister's shoulders. "I think that's enough for tonight, Sheriff. If you don't mind, I'd like to get my sister back to The Towering Pines and into her own bed."

Ruby raised her eyes to Victoria's. "And a hot bath."

CHAPTER

The Next Day
Bummers Gang Hideout

Dane rode beside Victoria as they followed Sheriff Peck and a wagonload of men to the cabin in Four Mile Gulch. The snow had begun falling early that morning, and the further they traveled the more the storm built with intensity. He pulled the brim of his hat low and tugged his wool scarf tighter around his neck. "Why were you so all fired set on comin' with us?"

Victoria, dressed in a dark suit and heavy outer coat, straightened in her saddle and pulled her fur hat down over her ears. "Sheriff Peck needs me up there."

Dane shook his head. "He even tried to talk you out of goin'."

Victoria kicked her horse into a gallop, leaving Dane several lengths behind.

The remainder of the journey, he let her have her space. But, it made no sense why the woman was so determined to travel to a cabin in the middle of nowhere.

Several inches of snow covered the hillsides before the storm quit and the sun appeared against a brilliant blue sky. Reaching the lone pine tree that Ruby had described, the sheriff turned and led the procession up the hill. Just as she had said, behind a rock outcropping they found the cabin, a corral filled with horses, and another outbuilding. Several empty wagons sat next to the cabin.

The sheriff dismounted and shouted orders. "You men feed and water those horses. Then hitch up those teams, tie the saddle horses behind. Load whatever you find in that outbuilding in those wagons."

Victoria pegged down her mare and hurried inside the cabin. She dumped a wooden box filled with jewelry onto the dirt floor, knelt on both knees, and sorted through the contents until she found the item for which she searched. She held a silver pocket watch by its long chain and tears filled her eyes. "She was right! It is his."

Dane knelt next to her. "Whose is it?"

A slight smile tugged at the corner of her lips. "It was our father's. After Ben proposed, I gave it to him." She ran her fingers over the intricate filigree design. "Ruby thought she'd seen it lying on the table." She held it to her chest. "I didn't think I'd ever see it again."

Sheriff Peck entered the cabin and whistled. "That is one pile of loot. What you got there, Miss Cashman?"

She grinned. "It's my father's pocket watch."

He took the timepiece from her, opened it, and read the inscription, "To my darling husband, Love Emma." He handed the treasure back to Victoria. "So how did the Bummers get it?"

Victoria grabbed Dane's arm. "This explains everything."

He laid his hand on hers. "What does it explain?"

"Don't you see?" She looked at the sheriff. "They killed Ben. They had to. It's the only way they could have gotten the watch. Ben loved this watch. He showed it to everyone."

The sheriff rubbed at the stubble on his chin. "They could have robbed him and stolen it. It doesn't prove they killed him."

Victoria squealed as she ran to the corner, picking up a pair of fine leather boots. "And these were Ben's too." She pulled a smashed, beaver-pelt hat from beneath the pile of clothing. "And this was his."

The sheriff examined the boots and hat and scratched at darks spots on both. "There's no doubt that's blood. You sure these were Ben's?"

Victoria nodded. "I'm positive."

He laid the clothing items to one side. "I'll be needin' those for the marshal."

Victoria held out the watch with a trembling hand. "Will you need this, too?"

Sheriff Peck folded her fingers around the precious heirloom. "I think we have enough with the boots and hat."

She slipped the watch into her pocket, and her attention went to the rock fireplace. "I almost forgot." She tugged at several large stones until she found one that was loose. Pulling it out and letting it smash to the floor, she reached inside the open void and hauled out handfuls of cash. "Ruby said she saw Bill put money in here."

"I'm sure glad you insisted on comin' with us, Miss Cashman." The sheriff said. "We'd never have found the money or those bloody clothes—and the watch. More than enough to hang them Bummer's for Rumson's killin'."

Dane nodded. "I feel pretty stupid thinkin' you crazy for wantin' to come along."

Victoria raised her chin and winked. "Let that be a lesson to you, Mr. Cholua. Don't ever question my motives when I'm determined to do something. It will only make you feel like a fool in the end."

Dane shook his head and muttered, "Women."

The remainder of the afternoon, Dane and Victoria assisted Sheriff Peck in collecting the gang's loot and loading it in the wagons. Meanwhile, the sheriff's men loaded the stolen dry goods and supplies from the outbuilding.

As the men drove away in the wagons, Sheriff Peck mounted his horse and tipped his hat. "Thank you again, Miss Cashman—and you too Dane."

Dane ducked his head in reply. "How you gonna sort out what belongs to who?"

"I got lists of things from the folks who reported the thievery and there's probably more I don't even know about." He blew air into his cheeks and then released it. "We'll need to get a list from the Cooper family. I'm sure some of this belongs to them."

"Big John loaned them a team and wagon this mornin' so they could get on up to Russell's Gulch before the storm got too bad." Dane said. "I'm not certain if Jake knows what they lost. I'll check with him."

"You do that." Sheriff Peck said. "Once I get the list, they can come by my office and collect their belongin's." He gazed into the distant horizon. "It's sure been an interestin' day, and I'm feelin' pretty good about bein' able to return some of those folks belongin's to 'em." The lawman pointed toward the mountains. "But, that sun is settin' fast and I'd like to get back to Central before dark."

Dane helped Victoria onto her mare and then mounted the horse he had borrowed from John. She pulled the watch from her pocket and a single tear slipped down her cheek.

"You go on ahead, Sheriff." Dane said. "We'll be along shortly."

He laid his hand on Victoria's shoulder. "I'm real sorry I doubted you, and I'm glad you got your father's watch back."

A smile tugged at one corner of her mouth as she wiped at her cheek. "And we solved the mystery of Ben's murder."

The nagging question in the back of Dane's mind refused to be stilled. He cleared his throat. "Do you still love him?"

"Ben?"

"You must have loved him a lot to have given that to him." He pointed at the watch. "Do you still have feelin's for him?"

She cupped Dane's chin in her hand, sending a dizzying current racing through him. "No! I do not love Ben Rumson."

She took her reins in her hands. "To quote you from a statement you made not too long ago 'We all have our moments of stupid.'"

As the icy winter moon rolled across the night sky, the couple rode into Black Hawk Pointe. Victoria tilted her head to one side. "Would you like to warm up with a cup of coffee before you head over to Miss Maggie's?"

Dane swallowed hard, trying to manage a feeble answer. She said she did not love Ben. But, how did she feel about him? Was her easy manner toward him just her way, or did she like him? Could she love him? Better to be safe than play the fool. "You probably want to check on Ruby and get some rest. I'll stop by in the mornin' before we head back up to the Hole in the Ground."

Overhead, the black ceiling of sky flowed with a million stars as brisk wind gusts rushed through the canyon. Dane pulled the collar of his jacket tighter around his neck. "Gettin' colder— Feels like more snow." His leg brushed against hers, sending a sensuous charge running through his body. "Good Night."

Victoria reined her horse to a stop and placed her hand on his forearm. "You're very good at avoiding the obvious, Mr. Cholua."

Dane hesitated only moments before his desires overcame him and caution was only a forgotten memory. He cupped Victoria's chin, searched her upturned face and then brushed his lips against hers. "Oh, Miss Cashman, I may not be a fine gentleman or well educated. But, I'm no fool." His kiss was slow and thoughtful. Then raising his mouth from hers, he gazed into her eyes. "Never assume you know what I'm thinking or feeling, Miss Cashman. It will only make you feel the fool in the end."

CHAPTER

13

Three Days Later
The Towering Pine Restaurant

Wearing a soiled apron over a cotton dress, Victoria stood in the kitchen doorway. She shook her head as she watched the spectacle before her. Angie and Timmy scrubbed the kitchen floor, sprays of soapy water splashed about, soaking the mother and son. In a stern voice, Victoria ordered Angie, "Get this mess cleaned up and then get out of those wet clothes."

Angie wrung her rag into the scrub bucket and stood. "I'm sorry. I guess we got a bit carried away." She dropped her arm around her son's shoulders. "I've been so happy since Timmy recovered, and we're feeling so blessed to be here with you—Well, I guess we got caught up in flipping water at one another, and I didn't realize what a mess we were making." She dropped back to her knees with a dry cloth, and began sopping up the water. "I'll have this cleaned up in no time." Angie looked up at her son. "Timmy, you get upstairs and change out of those wet things. Then go cut firewood and stoke the heating stoves."

Victoria stuffed a handful of soiled rags into the rag bucket. "I already stoked the fires." She swiped at her forehead. "Timmy.

Mr. Schmidt is looking for you. He said the stalls at the livery need mucking, the horses need fed, and he's busy with smithy work. Before you go, I used all the split wood, so chop some more and lay it in the rooms for later."

Timmy nodded. "Yes, Miss Vicki. I'll get right to that."

Ruby, wearing a powder blue satin gown, crossed the dining room and looked out the front windows. "What's got you in such a mood? I've never heard you talk to them like that. You usually reserve your Captain Victoria routine for ordering me around." She scanned the room. "Don't you have anything left to clean? Is that your problem?"

Victoria slumped into a chair at one of the dining tables. "Maybe you haven't noticed. I haven't had any customers for the past two days." She leaned her head back and groaned. "There's over a foot of snow out there, and it's still coming down."

Ruby laid a pile of cash on the table in front of her sister. "That should make you happy."

Victoria tapped her fingers on the money. "Well, it will go a long way toward paying the bills. Where did you get it?"

The younger sister ran a finger over a frosty pain of glass in the front window. "Isn't it strange how the weather keeps folks from eating at your restaurant? However, it never keeps them from doing what they really enjoy."

"I guess I've been so consumed with my own concerns, I hadn't paid any attention to the comings and goings through the backdoor."

Ruby went to the hall, stood in front of the mirror, and adjusted pins in her hair. "Now, maybe you can spend more time thinking about what's really bothering you and less time worrying about the restaurant."

"What do you mean?"

"You don't clean like this and get all contrary unless there's a man involved, and I'm guessing he's Dane Cholua."

Victoria bared her teeth and growled. "That man!" She dropped her head onto the table and moaned, "He kissed me."

Ruby hurried across the room and sat across the table from her sister. "Did you say he kissed you?"

"Yes!"

"When?" The younger sister giggled. "You're all worked up like this because he kissed you?" She smirked. "It's not like you've never been kissed."

The older sister stared straight ahead and pressed her palms to the table. "I've never been kissed like that."

"Oh, come on now, girl. More than a few men have romanced us in our lives. How can one kiss be so much different from any other?"

Thoughts like a soft and wispy cloud transported Victoria back to that night. She ran her fingertips across her mouth. Her mind burned with the memory of the kiss and his name lingered around the edges of her thoughts. "We'd just come back from Four Mile Gulch and the Bummer's hideout. The sheriff and his men had gone on ahead, and Dane and I rode in alone—just the two of us. We rode at a gallop most of the way and didn't have a chance to talk. When we got to the edge of town, we slowed down."

Ruby waved her hands in the air. "For heaven's sake, girl, I don't care about all that. The kiss! The kiss! Tell me about the kiss!"

Victoria rested her face on her cupped hand and sighed. "It was wonderful."

"And . . . ?"

"He bent across, took my chin in his hand and raised my face." She sighed again. "Then he kissed me real gentle like and brushed his lips across mine."

"And . . . ?"

"He said something about not being a fool—or something like that." She smiled and fluttered her lashes. "It was so beautiful."

Ruby slumped into her chair, her eyes wide. "Well I never . . ."

"Bet you never been kissed like that."

The younger sister giggled. "Oh! But, I have."

"You what!" Victoria straightened. "Who?"

"Well maybe not exactly like that. However, it was pretty special. Most men just grab you and kiss you hard on the lips—sometimes it's a little more than that, if you know what I mean."

"Yes, I know what you mean." Victoria laughed. "They seem to think the more passionate and rough they are the better we like it."

Ruby sighed. "Such fools."

"So who kissed you like that?"

Ruby wrinkled her nose, her blue eyes sparkling as she grinned. "Jake."

Both women rested their faces in cupped hands and sighed as Angie came into the room. "What are you two looking so starry-eyed about?" She rolled her eyes. "Oh, let me guess. Those Cholua Brothers. Right?" She sat in a chair between them, chuckled, and looked at one sister and then the other. "No doubt about it, you two got it bad."

The ladies laughed in unison. Timmy crashed through the back door carrying an armload of wood. "What's so funny?"

His mother shooed him away. "Oh, it's nothing, honey. Just girl-talk."

CHAPTER

Two Days Later
The Tollgate Saloon

Ruby stepped onto the wooden box Big John had set next to the wagon so she wouldn't muddy her shoes. The blacksmith lifted her from the box and stood her on the porch of The Tollgate Saloon. She tugged at the sides of her heavy coat and cleared her throat. "Thank you, sir. I think I can take it from here."

John rushed past her and opened the door. "I wouldn't be much of a gentleman, ma'am, if I didn't see you safely inside."

As they entered, she patted him on the arm. "John, we need to find you a good woman. All that charm and good looks is going to waste on me and Victoria."

"Oh, it ain't no secret you two are sweet on Jake and Dane. And I ain't the sort of feller who'd try to steal my best friend's gal."

She removed her coat and hung it on a hook by the door. "And who told you we were interested in the Cholua Brothers?"

The big man laughed. "It don't take no genius to figure that out." He bent down and whispered, "And just between you and me—I'm pretty sure they're sweet on you."

She whispered, "Just between you and me—let's keep that our little secret. Okay?"

A wide smile crossed his face. "Gotcha!"

Sam hurried from behind the bar and took Ruby by the hand. "My, Miss Ruby, we've sure missed you around here. Glad to see you're doin' okay."

Ruby removed her gloves and hat. "Well, I've missed you, too, Sam. I've kept in practice with our miner friends and—other businessmen in town." She winked at the bartender. "However, there's no place like The Tollgate for a little excitement."

Sam looked toward the staircase and scratched the side of his neck. "There's a woman upstairs says she knows you. I told her we don't allow ladies to stay here at The Tollgate. But, she showed up here a couple of nights ago in the middle of that storm and insisted she was stayin'. Couldn't very well turn her away under the circumstances. There weren't many customers— and she insisted." He sighed. "Quite a determined woman."

She raised an eyebrow. "Her name?"

"Belle Siddons."

Ruby gathered her skirt and hurried up the staircase. "Which room is she in?

"The one with the sign on the door." He huffed. "She put it there. I didn't."

Ruby passed by several closed doors until she came to the one with a note that read: *I've got a gun and I know how to use it.* She laughed and shouted, "Belle. It's Ruby."

The door flew open, and a beautiful woman with dark eyes and tousled chocolate curls greeted Ruby in a southern drawl. "Well, I swear it's about time you got here, girl. I've been cooped up in this room for the past two days waiting to see you."

The women embraced and Ruby grabbed her friend's hands. "What are you doing here?"

Belle laughed. "Get yourself on in here, and let's catch up. A lot's happened since you left New Orleans." She shut the door, braced a chair beneath the handle, and laid her pistol on the table next to the bed. She patted the mattress next to her. "Sit, girl."

Ruby hugged her friend once again. "How did you get here?"

"Like I said, a lot's happened. I was doing okay at the tables in New Orleans. Then, I got restless. So, I made my way across Kansas. I spent a few months in Wichita, then Ellsworth, then Fort Hayes. I ended up in Cheyenne, Kansas. That's where I heard about the gold strike here in Colorado, so I packed up all my winnings and headed to Denver."

Ruby furrowed her brow. "And you're in Black Hawk Pointe because . . .?"

Belle laughed. "Oh, don't worry, sweetie. I'm not here to gamble."

"Then why are you here?"

Her mouth dropped open. "To see you, silly."

With a sigh of relief, Ruby held her hand to her throat. "How did you know I was here?"

"You're quite a celebrity in these parts. Even down in Denver, they're talking about how you send those big city card sharks back down the hill with empty pockets and their tails between their legs." She winked. "And I heard you shot one of the men from the Bummer's Gang. You know he was still wearing a sling when they hung them. There was one big party in Denver on that day, let me tell you."

A sudden knock at the door interrupted the ladies' joyous reunion. Belle grabbed her pistol. "Who is it?"

"It's Sam. I was just wonderin' when Miss Ruby was gonna get started. Got quite a few customers downstairs waitin' to play."

Ruby opened the door. "I'll be right down, Sam." She glanced back at her friend. "You're welcome to join us."

"Let me get dressed and put myself together, and I just might find my way down there later this evening." Bell's dark eyes sparkled above an impish grin. "However, if you don't mind, I'd prefer to run my own table. I may have a better chance of walking away with my money."

Several hours later, Belle descended the staircase into the main bar room in a deep cut, dark green, taffeta gown, with her dark curls gathered over one ivory shoulder. The room went silent. Every eye was on her.

Ruby stood at the bar as her friend made her entrance, and they smiled at one another. "Gentlemen, this is my friend, Belle." Ruby said. "As a special treat, this evening, Belle will have a table back in the gaming room with mine. I'm sure you will find her as worthy an opponent as I."

A tall man in a grey, wool suit stood and removed his bowler hat. "Or as she's known in Denver . . . Madame Vestal." He gave Belle an icy stare. "I believe we have unfinished business, Miss Siddons."

An undercurrent of chatter filled the room as Belle raised her chin and glared at the man. "We have nothing to discuss, Mr. Jefferson." She turned her back to him and walked to Ruby, interlacing her arm with her friend's. "I'm in Black Hawk Pointe visiting my good friend, and she's invited me to host a table tonight. For anyone who is not familiar with my business in Denver, I run an honest gambling house in the city where we offer free drinks to our customers. Please feel free to stop by next time you're down that way."

Ruby pulled Belle up against her and whispered through clenched teeth. "Enough of the self-promotion." She smiled at the gentleman to whom Belle was speaking earlier. "Mr. Jefferson, it seems you and Belle may have some difference of opinion, and I certainly don't want you getting the wrong impression of our friendly town. You're welcome to join me at my table—if you like."

Belle's eyes grew wide and she shook her head. Ruby glared at her. "You go on in and get started, Belle. Mr. Jefferson and anyone else who'd like to join us at my table will be in soon."

Several hours later, Belle's table had cleared leaving her with a handsome stack of money. Ruby's game grew intense, leaving only her and Mr. Jefferson. He had won a number of hands.

However, now he was losing, and the gentleman grew agitated. Belle put her money in her reticule and headed for the door. As she passed Ruby, she bent down and whispered, "Get out of here, now."

Ruby scowled at her friend. She had no intention of skedaddling.

Jefferson stood. "You get outta here, and leave us be."

Belle left, and Jefferson took his seat. "Now, where were we, Miss Ruby?" He sent her the same icy stare he'd given Belle. "I believe you were about to pull the last card in the box—were you not?"

The lady drew the card and laid it face up. Jefferson had lost his bet. He turned over the table and grabbed hold of Ruby. "You're no better than that no account friend of yours." He pulled her to him and grabbed at her skirts. I'll take my money and a little piece of you too."

The door to the gaming room slammed open and Big John stood where the now shattered obstacle once hung. "Get your hands off her if you know what's good for you."

Jefferson tossed Ruby aside and went for his gun. Before he got off a shot, the blacksmith manhandled him to the ground. Pressing his huge forearm against the gambler's throat, John leaned in close. "You're going to leave here and you're never going to show your face in Black Hawk Pointe again."

CHAPTER

The Next Morning
Hole in the Ground Mining Camp

Dane tossed a handful of roofing shingles out the door of the
cabin. "Might as well use 'em for firewood."

Loaded down with an armload of splintered two-by-
fours, Jake groaned as he trudged through two feet of snow.
"Might be we could use some of these in the mine." He piled the
lumber alongside the cabin and shaded his eyes as he looked
into the cloudless blue sky. "Think we can get a roof on this
place before the next snowfall?"

Dane tossed another load of shingles onto the pile outside
the door. "No chance. We'd best plan on sleepin' in the tent or
in the mine for awhile. The tent leaks. And, I'm not crazy about
sleepin' in the mine. It might not be much dryer with all this
snowmelt."

Jake waved his hands in the air as he stared from inside the
cabin at the open sky. "Who'd of thought it would just cave in
like that?"

"I'm just glad we got out before it all came down on us."
Dane dropped his hands to his sides and looked up. "I was sure

we had enough crossbeams and I even used extra pegs in the supports."

"Looks like we need to get into town and get some more lumber and shingles if we're gonna get started."

Dane grinned as his thoughts turned to Victoria. It had been five days since he left her in front of The Towering Pines. Those first days cooped up in the cabin, she occupied his every thought. Around day three, the roof began creaking, and the snow came down so relentless they could not see two feet away from the window. The storm blew in threw small slits in the chinking and under the door, and all they could do was try to keep warm beneath piles of blankets. With the fireplace not yet completed, they survived on beef jerky, cold potato cakes, and canned beans.

Jake cleared away the snow from where he thought the fire ring had been. "If we get a fire going, we can at least boil some water and clean up before headin' into town."

Dane grabbed a shovel and began digging. "Good idea." He scrunched up his nose as he sniffed at his shoulder. "I'm thinkin' a meal at the The Towering Pines sounds mighty good."

"And a chance to see Miss Victoria and Miss Ruby wouldn't be unwelcomed either." Jake laughed. "Who you think you're foolin'? It's plum clear to me you're sweet on Miss Victoria. She's all you talked about them first couple of days we was up here."

Dane pelted his brother with a snowball across the back of his head. "And you don't care nothin' about Miss Ruby, now do you?"

Jake lit a fire under a stack of roofing shingles. He warmed his hands and tossed on a few more shingles while Dane formed another snowball, which he pelted at Jake's shoulder. The younger brother warmed his hands again, reached into a snow bank and formed a ball, flinging it at Dane and catching him on the left cheek.

"Ouch! That hurt."

"Warm hands add that special icy touch." Jake flung another ball at Dane, catching him in the shoulder. "Don't be such a baby."

For the next thirty minutes, a snowball fight commenced, stopping only when Dane dropped onto a snow-bank, breathless. "Okay. You win." He pushed himself upright and entered the cabin. He collected two pots, two scrub brushes, and two towels, and returned to the fire. "If we're gonna get into town before the sun sets, we'd best start cleanin' up."

Once the water came to a boil, they added snow to cool it down, stripped their clothes, and began scrubbing. As Dane stood next to the fire drying off, a loud growl came from behind the cabin. "You hear that?"

Jake wrapped his towel around his waist and ran toward the structure. "I sure did. That's a grizzly if I ever heard one."

Inside the cabin, the brothers bolted the door and pushed a table in front for extra weight. After barricading themselves inside, Dane grabbed his rifle.

Jake laughed and pointed at Dane.

"What's so funny?" Dane said. "That thing's gonna kill us."

"You do realize neither of us has a stitch on, don't you?"

"Bein' naked is the least of our worries, brother." He tossed a rifle to Jake. "At the moment, I'm more worried about gettin' eaten alive."

Jake continued to snicker as he stood next to the window and peeked out. The bear crashed through the glass, sending shards flying across the room. Jake's face went pale and he fired a shot, piercing the bear's paw, causing it to roar and throw itself against the cabin wall. The barrier creaked.

"Great!" Dane said. "Now we've got a wounded grizzly after us."

Jake slumped against the wall and buried his face in his hands. "Never thought they'd find me naked and dead in a cabin on the top of a mountain—mauled by a bear, no less."

A loud *crack!* thundered from outside, and the bear pulled his wounded paw from the window. Another *crack!* pierced the air, and the bear let out a deep squall. The wall of the cabin shuddered and creaked, then all was silent.

"Jake, Dane? You in there?"

Dane rose up and peeked out the corner of the window. "Big John? That you?"

The front door shuddered as the blacksmith pushed against it. He went to the window, looked inside and let out a hearty laugh. "If you two ain't a sight." Then he looked up. "Hey! Where's your roof?"

"Come on in," Dane said.

Jake scurried into a corner. Dane pulled on his jeans and boots, and pulled the table away from the door. The doorway stood empty. "John?"

Dane walked outside.

The blacksmith knelt next to the body of the grizzly. Though a broad grin crossed his face, he brushed away several tears. "Beautiful animal." He cleared his throat. "My first grizzly. Not many left in these parts."

Dane and John looked at one another, and an understanding passed between them only known by hunters. They hunted for food and hides. Like the Indians who hunted the territory before them, they had a deep respect for the creatures they hunted.

A woman's voice echoed from further away. "Is it safe to come up now?"

John rolled his eyes. "They insisted on coming along to make sure you two were alright."

Three women led horses, and Dane recognized Victoria and Ruby. "Who's with them?"

John's face reddened, and he stammered. "Oh—that's Miss Belle."

CHAPTER

With the assistance of the brothers and the ladies, John skinned the bear. At over six feet tall and weighing at least 800 pounds, there was no way they could move the creature to another location.

Belle pushed strands of dark curls away from her cheek, leaving a streak of blood. John wiped it away with a clean rag. "How is it you know how to skin a bear?"

"Actually, I've never skinned a bear before. However, I'd think it would be easier than removing a bullet from a man's gut."

Ruby excused herself several times since the skinning began. John had to give the lady credit, though, she kept returning to help. She pulled at the hide on the leg as Jake ran his blade between the skin and muscle. "Belle's husband was an army surgeon." Ruby said. "She assisted him in his surgery and he taught her to play cards."

John's heart sank. "You have a husband?"

"No. I'm a widow. Newton died of yellow fever before our second anniversary."

Stricken at the thought of her being widowed so young, the blacksmith intensified his attention to his work at hand. "I'm sorry. That must have been hard for you."

"Thank you. It was hard. At first, I was devastated over losing him, and I didn't know where to go or what to do to support myself. My family was in Missouri and we were in Fort Brown, Texas."

Dane stopped cutting away at the bear's left side. "You from Jefferson City?"

"Yes. Why?"

He resumed cutting, and gave John a knowing glance. "Our pa talked about a man from those parts named Siddons, and I thought you might be related—probably not the same family."

John set his knife aside. "Bet you miss your family, don't you?"

"Sometimes." She chuckled. "Mama would just die if she could see me now. She'd probably get the vapors if she knew I ran a gambling house."

Victoria sat back. "Do they know where you are?"

"They know I'm in Denver. They think I'm a school teacher. The last letter I got from Mama, she was saying how the war was getting' ugly, and I was probably better off not being in the states at all." She stood and picked up a pile of snow to wash the blood from her hands. "Well, that's done." She stared toward the west. "John, would you mind walking with me back to that spring we passed on the way up here? I'd like to get a drink of water and wash up a little more."

"We'll start cutting up the meat," Dane said. "You two go ahead."

Belle slipped her hand into the blacksmith's. He stopped walking and jerked back. "I'm sorry," Belle said. "You're such an easy man to be with, and I felt so comfortable. I guess I just assumed you were available."

He took her hand in his and walked on. "No, you just surprised me." His toe caught on something beneath the snow. He stumbled and pulled her down with him as he fell. "I'm sorry Miss Siddons. Are you okay?"

She laughed as she pushed herself up out of a snow bank. "I'm fine Mr. Schmidt."

Her ivory face held a rosy flush across her cheekbones, and her long dark lashes over those chocolate brown eyes gave him joy just to be near her. He lifted her from the snow and stood her upright, brushing the white crystals from her hair and shoulders. "Sorry, ma'am. That was right clumsy of me."

"Where are you from?" Belle asked.

"I was born and raised in Ohio. My family moved to Colorado to homestead back in '52, and we been here ever since."

"They live in Black Hawk Pointe?"

"Not too far. They got a farm over in Golden Gate Canyon."

She nodded. "It must be nice to have family close by."

John filled his canteen from the spring and then handed it to Belle. "Don't see much of 'em with runnin' the livery, my smithy work, and minin' with Dane and Jake."

After drinking a long swallow, she knelt down and washed her face and hands in the water. She shuddered. "Cold—but refreshing."

"Think you'll ever go back to Missouri?"

"Not until the war is over." She stood and wiped her face with her scarf. "You may as well know. We're southern sympathizers. It's not a popular position to be taking. However, it's where my family loyalties lie."

She took his hands in hers and gazed into his eyes. "You're a kind and sweet man, John Schmidt. Some lady's going to be mighty lucky to land you one day."

He exhaled a long sigh. "You're makin' it mighty hard for me to mind my manners, Miss Siddons."

Slipping her hand behind his head, she pulled his face closer to hers and kissed him. "I'm not used to being with a gentleman, and I'm not much of a lady. With all that's happened, losing Newton, the war and . . . well, with just everything going on in my life, I grab what joy God sends my way, and I'm thankful for it."

John stepped back and cleared his throat. "Mind if I ask what the story is with that feller last night? Seems he was none too happy seein' you at The Tollgate."

"Make no mistake. He knew exactly where I was. That's why he was there."

"What did you do to him that got him that riled?" He took her by the hand and headed back toward the cabin. "And why did he go after Miss Ruby like he did?"

"Mr. Jefferson is not a very good card player. However, he is an important man in certain circles, and he never likes to lose—not at cards, or in business, or politics."

"Will he be in Denver when you go back?"

"I hope not. It would be just as well for everyone if he went back to Missouri. However, I doubt he's going to give up until he gets what he wants."

John shook his head. "He wants his money back?"

"It's not that simple. He wants me to marry him and go back to Missouri."

The woman was an ever-changing mystery, and a little voice in John's head warned him to get as far away from her as possible. However, he was smitten with her southern drawl, those dark eyes set in thick, black lashes—and she liked him. After her last declaration, he was stunned speechless for a few moments. "And you don't want to marry him?"

"Heavens no! He's an impossible tyrant who thinks everyone should bow and scrape at his command. He only wants to marry me because he thinks it will get him closer to my uncle and further him up the political ladder." She huffed. "He threatened to follow me to whatever mud-hole I went to until I gave in, and he's not beyond physical abuse to get me to go with him."

John's mind swirled with the possibilities of what Mr. Jefferson might do to Belle. "Who's your uncle?"

"He was the governor of Missouri. My mother's family are large landowners and Uncle Claibourne is her brother. I was a teenager when he held office, and in order to introduce me to high society, he took me with him when he traveled. That's when Mr. Jefferson set his cap for me. When I married Newton, I didn't see him for a long while. I hoped he'd given up. However, not long after I arrived in New Orleans, he showed up at my table. It seems no matter where I've gone since, he's always there." She giggled. "Maybe I should hide out up here. He'd never dirty his boots climbing up that mountain."

CHAPTER

Next Day
Black Hawk Pointe

While Dane went to the mill to get more lumber and shingles, Jake visited the general store for supplies. "You're out of coffee?" Jake shouted. "How can you be out of coffee?"

The store clerk shrugged. "After Mr. Gregory quit makin' his special brew, folks been comin' in here buyin' up every bag of Arbuckle's I had."

"Why'd he quit makin' it? It was mighty costly, but it was a good cup of coffee."

"The way I hear it, he's sellin' everythin' and movin' back to Georgia. Says he made his fortune and he misses his family."

Jake picked up the wooden crate containing his supplies and headed toward the door. "Don't suppose you know if they got any coffee up in Central City?"

The man shook his head. "Nope. Already tried to get some from them. They're out too."

"When will you have more?"

The clerk scratched his head. "Can't say for sure. I was expectin' a delivery tomorrow from Denver. With that snow storm, and now this melt, can't say when the wagons will make it up here."

"Maybe I can borrow some from Miss Victoria until you get some more."

"The man behind the counter shook his head. "She ain't got none either. Angie came in yesterday lookin' for some."

Jake palmed several nuggets and chuckled. "A pocket full of gold, and I can't buy a cup of coffee. What's this world comin' to?"

As Jake opened the door, Hannah Cooper stepped inside. Baby CC cooed and smiled up at him with big brown eyes. Jake smiled and wiggled his fingers at the child. "She's lookin' happy this mornin'. How's the rest of the family, Mrs. Cooper?"

She blushed beneath her dark blue bonnet, setting off her blue eyes. She lowered her gaze, her blonde lashes brushing on fair cheeks. "Clayton is at the mill picking up lumber for my brother's store. It seems we keep running out of room to stock things since we started selling that coffee. He and my brother are adding on an extra room to roast and grind the beans. They said we need more storage space for the bags and such."

The store clerk's eyes flew open wide. "You got coffee?"

Jake echoed the man's reaction. "Yeah? Really?" Then he recalled the Coopers listing twenty bags of Brazilian coffee beans among the items the Bummer's gang stole. He set down his crate of supplies and reached out for the baby. Jake did not know a hill of coffee beans about taking care of children. He knew ladies, though. In addition, he knew ladies with babies loved to have folks fuss over them. "Can I hold CC for you while you do your shoppin'. She's such a beautiful child."

She gently laid her baby girl in Jake's arms and blushed again as she raised her eyes to meet his. "I'd very much appreciate that, Mr. Cholua. I only need a few yards of fabric and some thread. My brother just carries food items, mining tools, and such for the miners. My sister-in-law and I thought we'd make quilts—what with winter coming on and all."

71

Jake sat on a chair by the door, and though he felt awkward holding the squirming bundle, he smiled and nodded. "We'll be just fine right here until you're finished."

As she picked out her fabric and selected thread, the store clerk followed behind. "I don't suppose I could buy some of that coffee from you, Mrs. Cooper?"

She ran her hand along a bolt of red, blue, and white calico. "Two yards of this will do nicely. And maybe two yards each of the deep red and royal blue."

The clerk clasped his fingers as though begging. "The coffee—Mrs. Cooper?"

She picked up several spools of various colors of thread. "And I'll take these, too."

The clerk measured off her fabric, cut it, wrapped Mrs. Cooper's purchases in brown paper, and tied them with string.

She opened her reticule. "How much?

"The coffee?" The clerk said.

"How much for my order?'

The clerk narrowed his eyes and grinned. "How about we swap your order for say a dozen bags of ground coffee?"

"Sir, you will have to speak with my brother or my husband about the coffee. I have nothing to do with that nonsense. Gracious me, I don't even drink the stuff. Give me a good cup of tea any day." She held out several dollars. "Will that cover my order?"

His lips drew into a taunt line and he muttered, "Yes, ma'am."

Jake handed the baby back to her mother and reached for her parcel. "Let me take that for you."

Hannah smiled. "Well, thank you. You're so kind. I'm sure Clayton would like to see you. Why don't you walk over to the mill with me? He mentioned something just the other day about paying you for our meal and the room you so graciously paid for when we arrived."

Jake placed her order with his supplies. "That would be great!" He picked up the crate and opened the door, directing her through.

Once in the street, Jake glanced back at the general store. The clerk stood in the window glaring at him, as he walked away with Mrs. Cooper—and the coffee connection.

At the mill, Jake introduced the Coopers to his brother Dane and shared his dilemma of finding no coffee at the general store, as well as learning there was not an ounce of coffee available in Central City or Black Hawk Pointe.

Clayton Cooper arched his eyebrows and smiled. "If you don't mind riding up to Russell's Gulch, I'd be happy to give you enough to hold you over until the next supply wagon gets into town. We got plenty. Besides, I owe you."

Jake resisted the urge to shout, "Yes!" He shuffled his toe in the sawdust at his feet. "I guess I could do that." He raised his eyebrows to his brother. "Okay with you, Dane?"

"I hate to think of us goin' without coffee, so yeah, I guess so." Dane said. "How long you think it will take you to get up there and back?" He pointed to the wagon loaded with lumber. "We need to get back up the hill and get started on the roof as soon as we can."

Clayton took his daughter from Hannah and made silly faces at the child. "It's about an hour's ride up to our place. You're welcome to stay the night if you want, Jake."

"How about I help Dane get this lumber up to camp?" Jake said. "Then I'll come by your place later this evenin'. You sure it's okay if I stay the night?"

Hannah grinned. "Oh, it will be fine. My brother and sister-in-law have wanted to meet you ever since we told them about all you did for us."

All the way up the mountain, Dane grumbled and complained about Jake taking off on some fool's errand when he needed him the most. Nevertheless, once they hauled the lumber up the hill and stacked it, and Jake put away their supplies, he headed back into town.

As he rode through Mountain City, a group of people gathering in front of the Gregory Store caught his attention.

John Gregory was auctioning off his merchandise to the highest bidder. A few stacks of miner's gear and boxes of canned goods looked to be all that remained. Jake reined his team to a stop in the middle of the street, and climbed down from the wagon. "No coffee?" he shouted.

Gregory grinned and shouted back. "Been out of coffee for over a week."

Jake eyed a coffee roaster and grinder setting on the ground next to the entrance. "How much for those?"

Gregory shrugged. "How much you give me?"

"You're not selling them to the highest bidder?"

The mining mogul thrust out his chest. "How much you give me?"

A miner standing in front of Jake whispered. "Nobody wanted 'em. He already tried auctioning them off and got nary a bid."

Jake pulled two small gold nuggets from his pocket. "I'll give you these."

Gregory twisted the hair in his shaggy, red beard. "They're worth ten times that."

Jake shrugged. "Take it or leave it."

"Okay. You got a deal. But, you gotta load 'em in your wagon. And that roaster's a might heavy."

Several men helped Jake load the roaster, and then he loaded the grinder. As he climbed onto the seat and gathered the reins, he grinned down at the men who had helped him. "Next time I'm in town I'll bring you each a bottle of somethin' special."

The thought came to him several weeks earlier. Each Christmas, his mother made her special brew of coffee liqueur. It had a rum base, and she only used Brazilian coffee beans. He had been thinking how popular such a delicacy would be in the mining camps and local restaurants. Jake had no idea where he would get a grinder and roaster. He saw several cases of rum in Sam's storeroom at The Tollgate, so he had that covered. He needed Brazilian coffee beans, which he thought he might be able to find in Denver. He grinned as he thought of Dane's reaction when he showed up at camp. The older brother sent him to town for coffee. He would return with coffee beans, rum, the grinder and roaster, and Jake would have everything he needed to start brewing his coffee liqueur. He laughed aloud and said, "He'll probably just roll his eyes, walk away, and mutter something under his breath."

CHAPTER

Mid-November
Hole in the Ground Mining Claim

Dane swung his hammer with one loud *thunk!* driving in the last nail on the roof. He grabbed up his flannel shirt that lay beside him, and wiped sweat from his forehead.

Victoria carried a large pitcher from inside the cabin.

He leaned over the edge of the roof. "Hope you got some cold water down there."

She filled a glass. "Fresh from the spring." Shading her eyes, she looked up at Dane. "All finished?"

Dane nodded as he climbed down the ladder. "Yes!"

The sunlight percolated through the dense tangle of scrub oak and pine. "Last week we got three feet of snow." Dane said. "Now, it's so hot a feller would think it's August. Craziest weather I ever seen."

Victoria took a long drink from her glass. "I was thinking my business will probably slow down over the holidays due to winter weather. Now, I don't know what to expect."

He ran his fingers through her dark brown hair and swung her into the circle of his arms. Claiming her lips, he crushed her to him.

She looked around, and backed out of his grasp. "Dane! What are you doing?"

A wide grin filled his face as he again gathered her into his arms and held her snuggly. He whispered into her hair. "Ain't nobody around."

Her eyelashes fluttered against his cheek. "What about Jake and Ruby?"

He kissed the pulsing hollow at the base of her neck and brushed a gentle kiss across her forehead. "What about them?" He was as eager as an erratic summer storm. "Jake said something about going into town to get more rum."

She put her arms around his neck and buried her face into his chest, breathing a kiss there. She kissed his chin, and then pressed her lips to his, sending shivers of desire racing through him. He swallowed hard and whispered. "Victoria."

She sighed. "Yes."

He stepped back, releasing her from his embrace. Then he paced as he ran his hands through his hair. "I swear woman, you . . . ."

She giggled and then came up behind him, locking her arms around his waist. "Yes. I what?"

He broke loose from her grasp and headed toward the cabin, where he grabbed a pickaxe. Then he hurried off in the direction of the mine. "I need to break me some rock."

****

In the Cholua brother's cabin, Victoria started a pot of water to boil in the fireplace and descended into the root cellar, where she collected potatoes, carrots, and onions. After selecting a small piece of bear meat from the ice pit, she gathered it all into her apron and ascended the ladder. She stopped midway and

77

listened. Footsteps trampled on the wooden floor overhead. She smiled and said, "Feel better, now?" She exited the opening in the floor to come face-to-face with Ruby. "I thought you were Dane."

The younger sister shook her head. "He okay?"

Victoria giggled. "That's a matter of opinion."

Jake entered, carrying a brown glass bottle. He held it high above his head, his face beaming. "Our first batch!" He thrust his fist into the sky. "Yes!"

Ruby bounced on her toes, clasping her hands to her chest. "Oh, Victoria, it's just as delightful as Jake said."

Victoria pressed her palms to her cheeks. "That's wonderful. It should be perfect for after dinner."

Jake popped the cork on the bottle. "Oh, no!" He grabbed a tin cup and poured in a small amount of the dark liquid. "You're going to taste it now."

She shrugged, brought the cup to her lips and inhaled. "It smells amazing" She took a few sips. A smile tugged at the corners of her lips. "I must say, Jake, this is really good."

"So, you'll serve it at The Towering Pines, right?" Jake said.

He and Ruby grinned and both leaned in closer. "You will, won't you?" Ruby asked.

"I don't know. I've never served liquor in my restaurants before."

"But it's not liquor. It is *liqueur*. Many of the finest restaurants in the big cities serve *liqueur*. People will love it for after dinner at The Towering Pines."

Dane entered. With his eyes narrowing, his lips formed a tight line. "What are you . . . ." He sighed. "I thought you were going into town."

Jake shrugged. "Don't know why you'd think that."

Dane furrowed his brow. "Oh, never mind." His gaze went to the brown bottle on the table. "That what I think it is?"

Jake puffed out his chest. "Yep! Our first batch of Cholua's Coffee Liqueur."

"Our first batch? Oh, no." Dane said. "I ain't got no part of this crazy scheme of yours."

Jake dropped his arm across Ruby's shoulders. He pointed to her and then to himself. "Our first batch."

Victoria poured some into a cup and held it out to Dane. "Try it."

He took a sip. Then he took another sip. A grin formed on his lips. "That is good!" He slapped Jake on the back. "Tastes just like Mom's."

"You look surprised." Jake said.

"I have to admit, little brother. I didn't think there was any way you could make it work. But, you did it. Thought you were crazy when you built that shed up there and hauled all that stuff up the hill. A couple times, I thought you'd start a fire and burn down the forest, the cabin, and all. I'm not a man who won't admit when I'm wrong. And, I was wrong."

For the remainder of the evening, the couples enjoyed a good meal and several cups of Cholua's Coffee Liqueur. Ruby stretched and kissed Jake on the cheek. "I don't know about anyone else, but I'm ready to call it a night."

A full-sized brass bed sat on one side of the room and two cots on the other. The brothers had rigged a line and curtain to divide the cabin, just so there was a place for the ladies to stay when they came to visit. Victoria pulled the curtain across, leaving Ruby and her on the side with the bed. "Goodnight, gentlemen."

The brothers called back in unison, "Goodnight, ladies."

Several hours later, Victoria lay awake staring at the ceiling. She nudged her sister and whispered, "Ruby, wake up."

Ruby mumbled, "What?"

She had to know she'd made the right decision before she told Dane. "What would you think about me giving the claim Ben stole from Dane and Jake back to them?"

CHAPTER

19

Two Weeks Later
Denver

J ohn followed Belle into the enormous tent on Blake Street.
She turned to face him. "Welcome to Madam Vestal's
gambling den."

A sudden coldness hit the blacksmith's core. She escorted
him to the long mahogany bar on the far side of the enclosure.
Scantily dressed ladies served customers at a dozen gaming
tables.

"Step up to the bar, friends." Belle motioned toward Jake
and Ruby. "Don't be shy. We got the best whiskey and beer west
of the Mississippi. Step on up. Bob will take care of you."

Jake remained at the entrance, with his arms crossed over
his chest. Ruby stood at his side, her gaze darting back and forth
across the room.

John cleared his throat. "Not quite what I expected." He
locked eyes with Belle. "Are those women prostitutes?"

Belle let out a raucous laugh and laid her hand on his arm.
"Oh, come now, John. Surely, this isn't your first trip to the big
city."

He shrugged. "As a matter of fact, it is."

She held her hands to her chest. "Well, we do things a little different here."

He stepped back. "Are you . . . ?"

"A prostitute?" She laughed again. "Oh mercy, no! I make my living running this place and working the tables."

A young blonde woman, who could not have been more than fifteen-years-old, approached John. "Can I get you a drink, mister?"

His face grew warm. "No thank you."

Belle stepped away as the young woman laid her hand on the blacksmith's chest. "You're sure a good lookin' hunk of a feller."

He pulled at his collar and stepped back. "Thank you—I think."

The girl giggled and ran a finger down his cheek. "You new to town?"

John glared across the room at Belle. "Yes—Only here for a couple days."

The girl dragged her finger under his chin. "Well if you get lonely . . . I'm always here."

As the young woman walked away, Belle joined John at the bar.

"I think it's time for me to go." John said. He took several steps and then felt her hand on his arm. He turned to face her. "I need to leave."

"I'm sorry, John."

His heart grew heavy in his chest, and all activity around him moved in slow motion. He pushed her hand away. "It's not like I didn't suspect this was how you live. I hoped I was wrong."

John joined Jake and Ruby at the opening to the tent. He looked back at Belle one last time. "She's a beautiful woman, and she made me feel like I was special. It's just . . . I can't see me marryin' someone like her. She just ain't the marryin' kind."

Jake gripped John's shoulder. "Sorry, friend."

The blacksmith shrugged. "You must have thought I was a fool for takin' up with her."

"No, John." Jake said. "I understand only too well."

"She's a complex woman with quite a past." Ruby said. "It's part of what makes her so alluring. And, she's beautiful."

John's mouth formed a tight line. "Yeah, I guess."

He stared down the dusty street, watching wagonloads of people and supplies crisscrossing one another. Dirty men, women, and children huddled beneath tattered tents or sat in doorways of hastily built cabins, hunger and desperation in their deep-set eyes. The noise was deafening. The obnoxious smells of body odor mixed with manure and human excrement turned his stomach. Businesses hung shingles on half-finished wooden structures or in front of large, tattered tents. Across the street, a woman begged a well-dressed man for a few coins. John closed his eyes and shook his head. "Who'd want to live here? I don't get it."

Ruby clung to Jake's side, holding tightly to his arm. A mangy dog hiked his leg on a rock next to Ruby's skirts and she stepped back. "What are people thinking bringing their families to this horrible place?"

Jake shook his head. "Like us I guess. They thought they'd get rich and go back home with their pockets full in a year or so, or maybe homestead here." With Ruby next to him, and John on the other side of her, Jake led the way. "Let's just head back up the hill. We'll have to camp somewhere for the night, but we'll be back in Black Hawk Pointe sometime tomorrow."

Ruby stared at him, halting in her step. "What about the *liqueur*?"

"Have you seen anyplace around here that might serve *liqueur*? I ain't even seen a restaurant."

"We need to ask someone. I'm sure there's more to Denver than just Blake Street." A nicely dressed gentleman passed by and tipped his hat to Ruby. "There." She said. "Go ask him."

Jake released her from his side, and she slipped her arm through Big John's. The blacksmith laughed and laid his hand on hers. "I guess bein' second best is better than no lady on my arm at all."

"Oh, John. I am sorry it didn't work out with Belle. I didn't know things had grown that serious, or I would have told you."

John's pulse pounded in his temples as he raised his eyebrows. "Told me what? Did you know what she was doin' down here?"

She shook her head. "Oh, heaven's no! I thought she was working in a respectable establishment dealing cards for the house. That's what she's always done in the past. She said she owned the business. I had no idea she employed those girls or that the part of town she was in was so disgusting." Her jaw tightened and she glanced about her. "Belle is a southern sympathizer."

"I know that. She told me. But, I ain't got no dog in that fight. I mean, the north and the south and all that scrapping over slavery. Ain't nothin' right about one man owning another—no matter what color they are. But I've lived here most of my life, and I praise God that I don't have to go killin' my neighbor to prove anything."

Ruby sighed. "There's a lot more to it all than slavery. It's about land owners and economics and the such. Belle's family owns a great deal of land in Missouri, and the state is split between Union and Confederate sympathizers. Belle may be in Colorado for now, but at some point I have no doubt she'll return to her roots, no matter the danger."

"She said that Jefferson feller wants to marry her for political reasons. That got anything to do with all this?"

Ruby nodded. "Probably." She shrugged and laid her head against the big man's upper arm. "You don't need those kind of headaches." She patted his cheek. "One day you'll meet the perfect lady who'll make you a great wife, and you'll have a bunch of kids and live happily ever after in the canyons up the hill."

He chuckled. "You a fortune teller or somethin'?"

"No. I'm just a good judge of character. After playing cards with the best and the worst, I can tell you for certain I've learned to read people and their motives."

Jake and the gentleman conversed as Ruby and John joined them. Jake's eyes widened, and he wiggled his brows. "Mayor Moore, I'd like you to meet Ruby Cashman and John Schmidt." He turned to his friends. "This here is Mr. John C. Moore. He's the Mayor of Denver."

Ruby held her hand to her throat. "Oh, my! I guess I am a good judge of character." She nudged John in the side. "Mr. Mayor. It is an honor."

"Thank you, Miss Cashman." The man had a distinct southern drawl. "It is Miss, is it not?"

Ruby fluttered her lashes. "It is sir." Jake's jaw tightened.

"And, what is your interest in this liqueur Mr. Cholua is trying to sell me?"

She smiled at Jake and laid her hand on his arm. "Mr. Cholua and I are business partners—you might say."

The mayor lowered his chin and raised his eyes to meet Jake's. "I'd like to taste this liqueur of yours. If I like it, I'll buy a dozen bottles."

CHAPTER

The Towering Pines Restaurant
Black Hawk Pointe

Victoria served the customers while Angie kept the food coming. Timmy, dressed in his Sunday best, and wearing one of his mother's aprons, cleared away the tables and washed dishes. Every seat in the restaurant was full and remained so until well after eight o'clock in the evening. When the last customer left, Victoria dropped into a chair, folded her arms on the table, and lowered her head. "I can't believe we were this busy two days before Thanksgiving. I thought it would be slow."

Angie pushed back damp strands of blonde hair and slumped into the chair across from Victoria. "We are out of everything. And the supply wagon won't get here until next week." She shook her head. "I'm sorry, Victoria, but I'm afraid we'll have to shut down the restaurant until then."

Victoria tipped an empty brown bottle on end. "And we're out of liqueur as well."

"It is popular. Even the ladies like it. I think it's the French sounding name—*liqueur*." Rolling her tongue, she pronounced it with a French accent. "It is very good." She glanced toward the steps. "I sent Timmy upstairs after he finished the last of the dishes. Poor boy. With Mr. Schmidt out of town, he spent the entire morning at the livery and then he came back here and helped us. He must be exhausted."

Victoria reached into a pocket of her dress and pulled out a twenty-dollar gold piece. "That's a bonus for all your and Timmy's hard work. Buy yourself something nice, and get him something he wants."

Angie pushed the money back across the table. "I can't take that. You give us our room and board and pay me an honest salary. Sometimes we're busy and sometimes we're not, but you always pay me the same. That is more than fair."

Victoria slid the coin back. "If you don't take it, I'll give it to Timmy. I'm sure he'll take it."

Angie smiled as she picked up the money and stuck it in the pocket of her apron. "I'm sure he would." She laid her hand on Victoria's as she stood. "I'll see you in the morning. I think we still have a few eggs and a side of bacon, plus a few potato cakes. At least we'll eat a good breakfast."

"And coffee?"

The cook chuckled. "Yes, we have coffee. Mr. Cooper brought me a bag yesterday and we've still got a little left."

Victoria threw the lock on the front door. "Then I'll see you at breakfast. Make the coffee good and strong."

Angie called down from the staircase, "Just the way you like it."

As Victoria lowered the wicks on oil lamps along the walls and made her way to the backdoor, she gasped in shock to find a man standing in the back hallway. "I'm sorry, sir. If you're looking for Ruby, she's not here."

He came closer and glared at her with steely grey eyes. "Where is she?"

Victoria lifted her chin and opened the back door. "That is of no concern of yours. Please leave."

He grabbed the door and shut it with a quiet click. "Who might you be?"

"I'm Victoria Cashman, the owner of this establishment." She reached for the door handle, but he caught her by the wrist. She jerked free; and remembering her rifle was under the kitchen counter, she backed in that direction. "You will leave now!"

He lowered himself into a chair at the table nearest the kitchen, his eyes following her every move. "I wouldn't do that if I were you."

She moved closer to the counter and felt around underneath for her firearm. "What?"

He grinned. "It's not there."

Victoria dropped to her hands and knees and found the space empty. "What do you want?"

He picked at his teeth with a silver toothpick. "I have some unfinished business with Ruby."

As Victoria walked into the dining room, she picked up a sharp knife from the kitchen sink and hid it in the folds of her skirt. "Like I said, she's not here."

He sniffed. "Then I'll wait." He kicked back the chair opposite him. "Sit!"

Victoria's legs tightened, and every muscle in her body was ready to run. "You can't come in here and order me around."

She stepped closer to the staircase. She could not leave Angie and Timmy alone here with this lunatic. She had no idea what he had done with her rifle. Could she kill a man—even in self-defense? She was uncertain.

She tried a different approach, and sat opposite him. "Alright, I'm sitting. Are you going to tell me your name?"

"Jefferson."

She worked to hide the quiver in her voice. "And Mr. Jefferson, is it money you want from my sister? If so, how much does she owe you? I'll be happy to give it to you, and you can be on your way."

He spit on the floor, leaned his chair back, and plopped his filthy boots on the crisp, linen tablecloth. "Not money. Information."

She withheld her desire to shove his feet from the table and plunge the knife into the man's heart. "What kind of information?"

"When's she coming back?"

"I have no idea. She left yesterday to travel with friends, and she said she'd be back in a few days." She shrugged. "That's all I know."

He was at her side in seconds, his hands encircling her throat. "Friends, hey. One of those friends wouldn't be Belle Siddons, would they? Where did you say they went?"

In one desperate move, Victoria plunged the knife at his chest, missing and cutting through his upper arm. Blood spurted from the wound, sending crimson stains onto the tablecloth and Victoria's white, silk blouse. She released the knife and ran for the stairs. She screamed, "Angie, Timmy."

Jefferson reached for Victoria, ripping the edge of her skirt. She lunged forward on the steps. A loud *pop!* rang out. Something whizzed past her head.

Jefferson staggered and then fell backward down the steps, a gaping hole in his forehead oozing blood.

As Victoria looked up at an ashen-faced Angie holding a rifle, her vision blurred with tears.

Timmy stood behind his mother, his eyes wide and mouth agape. He cried out, "Is he dead?"

As Victoria made her way down the stairs, her mouth went dry, and her heart raced. She felt for a pulse on Mr. Jefferson's neck.

Angie joined her employer and told Timmy, "Go get Sheriff Peck."

Victoria laid her hand on Angie's. "No. It's too late. I don't want Timmy going all the way to Central City alone at this time of night. I'll go get the sheriff in the morning." She pulled the bloodstained tablecloth from the table and draped it over Jefferson's face and upper body. "Let's try to get some sleep. Tomorrow is going to be a very long day."

CHAPTER

The Towering Pines Restaurant
Next Day

Victoria descended the staircase to the aroma of bacon and eggs frying and coffee boiling in the kitchen—Mr. Jefferson lay where they left him the night before. Angie had covered the body in clean sheets, but blood had seeped out from beneath the linen, coagulating on the wooden floor. Victoria's stomach churned at the sight, and the tantalizing fragrance of breakfast lost its allure. She grabbed her hat and coat from the hall and hurried toward the back door. "I'm going for the sheriff."

Angie held a plate of bacon, eggs, and potato cakes in one hand and a cup of steaming coffee in the other. "Don't you want to eat first?" Her gaze went to the sheet-covered corpse. "I'd hoped by hiding him better, we'd at least be able to eat our breakfast."

Angie set the plate and cup on one of the tables. With her hand over her mouth, she ran out the back door.

Following behind her cook, Victoria then headed for the enclosure where she kept her mare. As she saddled the horse, she kept her attention on Angie. "Are you going to be alright?"

The woman sat on the back step with her head between her knees. She raised ashen cheeks beneath dark circled eyes and stared. "I just need a few minutes."

Leading her horse behind her, Victoria went to her friend's side. "Thank you."

Angie's voice came out in a near whisper. "For what?"

Victoria mounted and reined her horse away from the back of the building. "For saving my life."

"Oh, that." The cook wiped her face with a damp cloth and stood. "Yeah, well, I never killed a man before. I'm sure glad I had a husband who taught me to shoot. He said I'd never know when it might come in handy." She opened the door, stepped inside, and then turned to face Victoria. "Guess he was right."

An hour later, while the undertaker collected Mr. Jefferson, Sheriff Peck stood in the doorway of The Towering Pines. "I'm a little confused, Miss Cashman. You told me in my office the man attacked you, and you shot him."

Victoria nodded. "That's right, Sheriff."

Angie gasped and Timmy's eyes grew wide. Victoria glared at both of them. "When I realized his intentions were to get to Ruby to find out what she knew about Belle, and he wasn't leaving until he talked to her, I felt threatened and grabbed a knife from the kitchen."

"And you say he tried to strangle you?"

She unbuttoned the top two buttons on her blouse and showed him the bruises from Mr. Jefferson's hands. "Yes."

"And that's when you stabbed him?"

"Yes."

The lawman looked at Angie. "Did you hear anything?"

Angie looked at Victoria and then at the sheriff. "I heard loud voices. It sounded like Victoria was chasing off one of Miss Ruby's customers." She looked at Timmy, her mouth forming a tight line. "Timmy went to sleep as soon as his head hit the pillow. We had a very busy day. We all were exhausted."

Carrying Mr. Jefferson on a wide board, the undertaker and his assistant exited the restaurant. Sheriff Peck stepped aside to allow them to pass and then went to the staircase. He climbed the stairs and with slow steps descended. He stared at the bloodstained floor. He pointed up the staircase, then at the blood pattern on the floor. Victoria recalled that the blood splatter and brain matter from the gun shot had landed on the tablecloth she used to cover the corpse. "Is there a problem, Sheriff?"

"You said he took your rifle."

Her breath caught. "Did I say that?"

He nodded. "You told me in my office that is why you picked up the knife. You said that Mr. Jefferson told you he hid your rifle."

She stood holding her arm at her elbow and biting her bottom lip. "If that's what I told you . . . Yes, that's right. He took my rifle."

Sheriff Peck threw up his hands. "You see, that's my problem. How could you shoot him if he took your rifle?"

Angie stepped forward and shouted. Tears streamed down her face. "She didn't shoot him. I did."

Victoria tossed back her head. "Angie, no!"

"I heard the whole thing. When I realized Victoria was in trouble, I told Timmy to hide under the bed. I took my rifle and started down the steps. Before I was halfway down, Victoria came running up the stairs with Mr. Jefferson right behind her."

Sheriff Peck nodded. "Did he have a gun?"

"I don't know." The petite woman dropped into a chair. She lowered her face into her hands. "How was I to know if he had a gun or not? He had a bloody knife, and he was jabbing it at Victoria."

The sheriff sat across from Angie. "That's all I need to know." He patted her on the hand. "It's obvious to me—now that I have the real story . . . ." He furrowed his brow and glared at Victoria. "Miss Angie, you were protecting yourself, your son, and Miss Cashman from a man with a knife. It don't matter if he had a gun."

Tears rolled down Timmy's cheeks. "Are you takin' my ma to jail?"

Peck now stood in the open doorway to the restaurant. "No, son. She did what any good mother and friend would do. She protected what was hers. No crime in that." He looked at Victoria with a smirk. "Next time, just tell me the truth."

She shrugged and held out her palms. "Sorry. It's just that I have a feeling someone is going to come looking for Mr. Jefferson, and I didn't want Angie involved. I'll have to ask Ruby about him when she gets back."

"Where is she?"

"They went to Denver to try to find someone there who could sell their liqueur, and they were escorting Ruby's friend, Belle, back to her gaming hall. As I understand it, she was fearful of traveling alone. She said something about someone following her and the man being dangerous."

Sheriff Peck stepped back inside. "Jefferson?"

"It could be him." Victoria shrugged. "I don't know anything more about the man than what I've told you."

As the afternoon passed, the sky grew a threatening grey and snow began to fall. Victoria watched out the window for her sister. She paced the room and rehearsed what she would tell about Mr. Jefferson's demise.

Several hours earlier, she sent Angie and Timmy to Central City to buy whatever groceries they could find, and hopefully a turkey for dinner the next day. Even if she closed the restaurant to customers, they needed a Thanksgiving meal. She wrung her hands as she waited for someone to come.

The sound of a wagon pulling up drew her to the front door. She rushed outside without looking out the window and found Jake helping Ruby down from the wagon. Both their eyes twinkled with merriment, and they laughed as they chattered something about getting rich from the coffee liqueur.

Victoria threw herself into Jake's arms and wept. All the pent-up fear and anguish over the events of the night before came rushing out. She pointed toward the open doorway. "A man came . . . I stabbed him . . . there was so much blood . . . Angie shot him."

She sobbed as Jake, with his arm around her shoulders, led her inside. He sat her on a chair close to the door, and Ruby knelt at her feet. Jake walked to the bottom of the steps where an enormous dark spot stained the wooden floor. He pointed to it with his eyes opened wide. Ruby held her sister's hands in hers. "You have to calm down, Victoria. What happened?"

A few moments later, another wagon pulled up. Angie entered carrying a turkey. Jake stood at the bloody spot, his mouth agape. Victoria could not stop staring at the place where Mr. Jefferson had bled out.

Ruby handed her a napkin. "Blow your nose and calm down."

Timmy came in carrying a box of produce. "Hey, Miss Ruby. Mr. Jake."

As the boy disappeared into the kitchen, Jake shook his head. "Is someone gonna tell us what happened?"

Over the next hour, Angie, Timmy, and Victoria each told their version of the previous night's events. Ruby took a deep breath, held it in, and then paced. "This is all Belle's fault. If she'd never come here, Jefferson wouldn't have followed her. She broke Big John's heart, and now she nearly got my sister killed." She looked at Timmy and Angie. "And, he terrorized you two."

Dane entered, carrying a bulging cloth bag and two brown bottles. The tension in the room was so obvious it could not be ignored. He went to Victoria. Now, recovered from her previous outburst, her body ached and her swollen eyes burned. She reached out to him, "Dane?"

He knelt before her, "Yes."

"I love you."

94

CHAPTER

Thanksgiving Day
The Towering Pines Restaurant

Victoria worked with Dane into the early hours of the morning scrubbing the bloodstain out of the floor. A shadow still showed through, but it was much less obvious. She brushed strands of hair away from her face as she sat. "I wish it was that easy to wash from my memory."

Dane massaged her shoulders.

She leaned back and closed her eyes. "Oh, that feels so good."

"How's Angie doin'?"

Victoria sighed. "I'm not sure. She's a strong woman. I don't imagine killing a man is something you ever get over." She patted Dane's hand. "I owe her my life."

"Yep."

"And, there's just no way to repay someone for something like that."

"Just be her friend. And never forget what she did for you."

The clock struck four and footsteps padded down the stairs. Angie wrung her hands. "You two still up?" She looked at the wet floor and smiled. "Thank you."

Victoria wrapped her arms around her friend. "No. Thank you."

That afternoon, Big John, Miss Maggie, a young woman, and two boys joined the Cholua brothers, Victoria, Ruby, Angie, and Timmy at the Towering Pines.

Victoria's heart nearly burst with joy over the gathering of friends and family on such a special occasion. It was her first Thanksgiving in her business, and everything was perfect. Aromas of roast turkey and pumpkin pie filled the restaurant.

Dane pushed his chair away from the table and rubbed his stomach. "Angie, that's the best Thanksgiving meal I've had since we left Chicago."

From the far end of the row of tables, the petite cook beamed. "Thank you, Mr. Cholua. It's kind of you to say so." She laid her hand on Timmy's. "It's wonderful being here with all of you. I was an only child, and my husband and I just had Timmy. So, I never had a chance to share a holiday meal with so many people."

Big John went into the kitchen. When he returned, he had a tray of shot glasses, each containing a generous amount of Cholua's Coffee Liqueur. He put the tray in front of Jake. "I'm thinkin' you got somethin' to say."

Jake grinned as he distributed a drink to each adult guest and raised his glass. "It seems everyone important in my life, other than our ma and pa and our brothers and sisters—well—anyway—you're all real important to me. He offered his hand to Ruby, and she stood next to him. "As you all know, we started making this special liqueur, and we've been traveling around to get folks in other towns to try it." He sighed. "Yesterday, before the storm set in, a feller from Denver caught up with us and said there were folks back there wantin' our liqueur." Jake arched his brows and rolled his eyes. "Well, the mayor of Denver served it at a dinner, and yesterday he ordered fifty bottles. The man said he'd be back next week to pick it up, and he'd probably have an order for fifty more."

Dane raised his glass. "To Cholua's Coffee Liqueur."

A loud cheer went up from the table. "That's wonderful," Victoria said. "Although, I will admit I was hoping for an announcement of matrimony."

Jake smiled down at Ruby. "I'm not ashamed to say in front of all of you that I love this woman with all my heart. The time's not right yet."

"Jake's right." Ruby said. "Now, isn't a good time for us to consider setting up a home and starting a family." She held his hand in hers. "However, I do love him."

The winter storm that began the night before continued with fierce winds that howled around the doorway, rattling the front window. Over three feet of snow had fallen since it began, and the wintery blast showed no sign of letting up anytime soon.

Victoria stood. "I also have an announcement to make." She smiled at Dane and then at Jake. "I've been waiting for the right time to share this. Now, with all of you here, seems to be that time." She handed several papers to Dane. "I've decided to give my claim on the ground stolen from the Cholua brothers back to its rightful owners. Do with it what you will, gentlemen?"

Dane accepted the documents, and tipped his glass to Victoria. "And we accept your generous gift." He fingered the paperwork. "Although, I will admit it comes as quite a surprise."

Dane opened the papers, read them and then handed them to Jake. The younger brother smiled and shook his head. "Thanks, Miss Victoria. That's mighty kind of you."

Dane rubbed his chin and read through the papers again. "Yes, thank you." He took her hand in his. "You didn't have to do this."

"I know. I wanted to."

He scratched at his neck. "When the weather breaks, how about you put on those fancy duds of yours and join me at the creek?"

She smiled. "It's a date."

Conversations resumed around the table. Victoria had joined Miss Maggie, and was filling her in on the incident with Mr. Jefferson when John joined them. "I've not yet met your guests."

The older woman's lips turned up at the corners in an impish grin, and she winked. "You haven't met Katy and the boys?"

The blacksmith's ruddy cheeks took on a rosy hue. "No ma'am. I've been out of town for a couple of days, and it looks like I missed the arrival of several important people." He smiled at the boys and then at their pretty, red haired mother. "I'm John."

Miss Maggie patted his hand. "John Schmidt, I'd like you to meet my niece, Katy, and her sons, Billy and Charlie."

John took Katy's hand in his. "Nice to make your acquaintance, ma'am." Then he shook the boy's hands. "And you fellers too."

The boys both grinned, and Billy made an effort to say something around the pumpkin pie filling his mouth. John held up his hand. "No problem, Billy. I appreciate good pie, too."

As the clock chimed seven times, Victoria said her goodbyes to Miss Maggie, her niece and great-nephews. Once they were bundled in their coats, boots, and hats, Victoria opened the door. Snow blew in with such intensity, the flames in the oil lamps blew out.

John grabbed the door and forced it closed. He wiped frost from the front window and stepped back. "I don't think anyone's going anywhere tonight." He pointed toward the icy pane. The guests gathered and stared outside. "It's got to be six feet deep out there." John looked at Miss Maggie. "Don't think we can even get you across Gregory Street."

Victoria gasped when a loud creaking sound, followed by a vibration of the building, sent Dane running upstairs. He called down. "Jake! John! I left six, ten-foot boards next to the back door. Go dig them out and bring them up here."

The clock struck ten before the three men reappeared in the dining room. "That should hold it," Dane said. "I knew that sound too well, but Jake and I didn't have any way to brace the roof of the cabin before it came down."

John chuckled and opened his mouth to speak, but Dane glared at him. The big man was the only one who knew about Jake and him being trapped inside the cabin without a stitch on. And, Dane intended to keep it that way.

The blacksmith worked his jaw. "I was just going to say, it's lucky you had those boards out back." He grinned at Dane. "I am a might curious, though, why they were out there."

"I can only say it was an act of providence." Dane said. "There were some we didn't need when we fixed the cabin roof. When I brought them into town to return them, the mill was closed and Victoria told me to leave them out back, and she'd have someone drop them off."

Victoria wrapped her arms around Dane's neck, and kissed him square on the lips. "My hero!"

Dane blushed. "Ahh shucks, ma'am!"

Ruby and Angie carried stacks of pillows and blankets into the dining room. "We've only got three bedrooms upstairs, so we ladies will take those beds." Ruby said. "Gentlemen, it looks like you're sleeping down here."

Victoria relit the oil lamps while Angie poured coffee for everyone. Angie counted heads in the rooms. "I could use some help with breakfast in the morning. I start at four am. Do I have any volunteers?"

Everyone moaned.

Angie grinned. "We can thank Dane for bringing that bag of coffee. It looks like we may be here for awhile."

Dane smacked his forehead. "Oh, yeah. I plum forgot. I wanted to ask Jake if maybe he should start sellin' coffee as well as the liqueur. Seems folks around in these parts drink a lot of that Arbuckles stuff; and it might be they'd buy Jake's coffee instead, seeing how they know him personal like, and they don't have to wait for the supply wagon to get to town before they can get more." He smiled at Jake. "You could even put it in small packs for the miners like Arbuckles does."

"Well, darn it, Dane." Jake said. "That's a great idea." He looked at Ruby. "Why didn't we think of that?"

"Don't know," Ruby said. "But it sounds to me like you may not have much time for mining if you're going to keep Black Hawk Pointe, Central City, Denver, and every little gulch around here in coffee—and liqueur."

THE END

BONANZA BEANS

Book 3

Release date: Fall 2015

Maggie Magoffin is a columnist, short story author and novelist with a Bachelors Degree in English and Professional writing.

When she's not entertaining her readers with a novel perspective of the old west, she's most likely traversing the spiraling back roads of her Colorado foothills.

Visit Maggie at www.maggiempublications.com.

www.ingramcontent.com/pod-product-compliance
Lightning Source LLC
Chambersburg PA
CBHW020153180626
46810CB00004B/1881